WHERE THE GREEN STAR FALLS

WILLIAM JACK STEPHENS

Sterling Adventure Group, LLC

CONTENTS

Be The Story

The most enjoyable part of my life is sharing my stories. Everything I write about has elements of things I've actually experienced, places I've seen, and people I've known. Sometimes it's the grittier side of life, and sometimes it's all about the beauty. It could all be real. If this sounds like what you enjoy reading, we need to connect.

Stay In Touch - Almost every month I like to discount some of my books, or even give one away for Free. I send a message to everyone on my **Mailing List** when the discounts are about to happen. I also let people know about New Releases.

You can sign up to the mailing list here: **Mailing List Sign Up**

Or at my website: www.williamjackstephens.com

A Journey To Fate

We all live under the veil of a little lie we tell ourselves. That we have absolute control of the world that surrounds us. That we shape it and mold it with our thoughts and our will and wishes, as if all that exists resides within a little bubble of space that spans only our visible horizon. When we move, it moves with us, and when we exert our force of will, it complies. The universe is what we think it is, and we control our own destiny.

It was the most innocent of mistakes, a simple miscalculation actually, that was about to send the life of Nicholas Azzarà out of control and destroy the lives of everyone he loved. The universe had something completely different in mind for Nicholas, and it was about to push him outside the boundaries of his perception of the perfect life. Whether he kept on living, or not, would be up to him.

"Marie, we need to leave now, por favor!" he bellowed as he stood next to the open front door, alternating his gaze between his Omega watch and the winding staircase leading up to the second floor. "The sun will be up in thirty minutes, and we need to be out of Buenos Aires before daybreak."

His wife, Marie, was oblivious to his impatience. She'd seen this side of him many times. Nico was driven. He was obsessive. He lived his life as if it were one long, unending mission, and failing to meet even the smallest deadline would have life-altering consequences. He wasn't born that way. When he was young, all he really wanted to do was be out on the river with his father. But life has a way of detouring young men away from their passions, like fishing.

"Nico, your screaming won't make us move any faster," she said in a calm, mastering voice. "Why is it so important that we get out of the city so early?"

"Because eleven people were killed two days ago, Marie. And some of them were just children. Have you forgotten the bombing in the restaurant just five blocks from here already?" Then he glanced at his watch again, and tapped the crystal three times as if it might have stopped working and a few taps would bring it back to life.

"I haven't forgotten the bombing, Nico. But what has that got to do with us? We're not a part of all that." Marie said.

"No one is safe right now. They don't care if you're

involved or not. I just want to get you and Cristian out of here safely, so if we leave now, we can be in the mountains on the other side of the country before the sun goes down tonight, laying in the green grass and drinking wine. Please, just get in the car."

These were very dark days in Argentina. It was 1979, and just a few years before, the military junta had successfully seized control of the government in a coup d'état. The rising leftists and Castro-backed communists were wreaking havoc, killing, kidnapping, and bombing public buildings, hotels and restaurants. The last thing Isabel Martinez de Perón did in her brief and weak stint as president was sign the "Annihilation Decrees" to hunt down the leftist guerrillas and anyone associated with them.

Buenos Aires became a fearful place for everyone; activists, unionists, journalists, teachers, rich and poor alike. Everyone. It was a chaotic and violent time in one of the most rich and beautiful cities in the world.

Buenos Aires was the fashionably fabulous southern cousin of the cultural centers, all rolled into one. More Parisian than Paris; more Roman than Rome, with endless cafés along tiled walkways in the shopping districts and towering architectural marvels of stone-carved office buildings and apartments. There were barrios with names like Recoleta, Palermo, and Chinatown; it was a microcosm of the most interesting influences the world had to offer. Plazas, parks and squares in every corner of the city brought people together to relax and mingle. The wide avenidas offered circling views of monuments and statues of generals, presidents, and Greek mythological legends with rotondas to spin the traffic in elegant spheres without the hindrance of stoplights.

Nicholas, Marie, and their young son Cristian, were about to make the long drive to their annual vacation in the mountainous forests of Patagonia. It was mostly business for Nicholas as he owned a great deal of property there, but the raging violence in the city had him unnerved, so he was eager to slip out under the cover of darkness while the streets were empty. Marie and Cristian loved the trips every summer, and treasured the landscapes and wilderness of the southern Andes mountains.

NICHOLAS, or Nico, as his family and friends called him, had the life that many dreamed of in his South American home, keeping his family in the well regarded barrio of Recoleta. He was the son of an Italian immigrant, like many millions of others whose families fled to this southern haven after the end of the second great war in Europe to escape starvation and hardship. His father, Gerard, had once been a fine furniture craftsman in Turin, Italy near the French frontier, making the most stylish and comfortable chairs that adorned the great halls of influentials.

Nico was tall like his father, but without the muscular frame of a man who makes his living with his hands and his back, and he had his mother's olive skin and wavy hair that were authentically Italian. He carried himself with a confident stroll, but not the kind of confidence that seeps from a man who has done and seen and made his own way. That's the kind of man who walks his path with no need of his voice to tell the world who he is, because the world sees him coming plainly enough, and it knows him.

Nicholas didn't yet possess that kind of confidence. He was confident like a young man who still needs to hear his name announced when he enters a room and craves the immediate attention of everyone inside. Confidence that requires resupply by fashion, and friends, and envy, and the approbation of beautiful young women. He was a young man who still had need of his own voice, and yet, he had talents and dreams, and strength that one day might find their way to the surface.

Nico lacked his father's artistry for woodworking, but as he grew up in the streets of Buenos Aires he became a shrewd navigator in the business world, and he had leveraged his father's small back-alley furniture shop into a titan of industry in South America. First by landing influential clients for his father to build unique pieces of furniture that would be seen by other wealthy patrons, and then by leveraging those contacts to finance a larger factory and the big commercial contracts that came with them. The banking and financing assistance that became available to him after he married, allowed him to expand the business and acquire assets. He and his family were now worth an incredible fortune.

Where he had once chased the lumber trucks through the industrial part of the city as a boy, picking up scraps of wood for his father to carve into a meal for the family, he now owned the largest lumber mill in Argentina, a large furniture factory and the small custom shop his father started, and much to his delight, over 300,000 acres of timberland in the Andes mountains of Patagonia for his own raw material supplies. He lived like a proverbial king.

To validate his success, he had also married well. His wife, Marie, was Buenos Aires royalty. Her parents came from well connected political families, and one of her french immigrant ancestors had married into the family of General Jose de San Martin, the lineage of Argentina's most famous military hero, and the man who helped free Argentina from the grips of Spain. The small town in Patagonia, San Martin de Los Andes, that they were driving to today, was named after her great great great grandfather.

* * *

NICO WAS HOPING to make the perimeter of the city before it turned into eight lanes of creeping, honking, and smelly fumes, so he rushed Marie and the boy to gather their bags and bodies into the champagne silver Mercedes 300D before the sunrise. Cristian fell instantly back to sleep stretched out on the rich leather rear passenger seat, and Marie pushed back slightly to extend her long legs and slipped off her heels for the hours of driving ahead. She opened the window just an inch to feel the cool morning air on her cheeks, which annoyed Nico because he bought the new 300D for the luxury and comfort of things like fine German air conditioning.

They left thirty minutes late of his planned departure time, and he drove rapidly through the barrio lined with garden homes enclosed by high walls draped in blooming bougainvillea and crested iron gates; then past the sea port, which was always busy with container trucks entering and leaving, no matter the time; past the grand cemetery where most of Argentina's heroes were laid to rest, and onto the highway that would take them due west to the Andes mountains.

The shield of darkness was lifting as they neared the edge of the city and the landscape changed to gently rolling hills, and suddenly to endless waves of green pastures and the country estates of the privileged. A translucent early morning fog hovered over fields of knee high grass and alfalfa and manicured polo fields, and Marie woke Cristian just in time to see the magnificent horses grazing beneath broad shading roble trees.

"Cristian, wake up and see the horses," Marie said.

"When we get to San Martin I'm going to teach you how to ride, and we'll do a long adventure up to Chapelco Mountain on horses, just the two of us. It's so high you can see all the way to the Pacific Ocean."

"Papa is going to teach me to fly fish this year, he promised!" Cristian said, then he slid forward on the edge of the seat and leaned up between the two front bucket seats so he could see his father's face, and Nico glanced back and smiled, and said, "I think I can make time this year." Fly fishing was a tradition in the Azzarà family, and Cristian had grown up hearing about the adventures of his father and grandfather out in the wild places.

Cristian bounced back into the seat with a happy grin, then slid to the left and pressed his face against the glass to see all the horses as they passed through the farm country. Thoroughbreds, polo ponies, silvery black Andalusians, and uniquely Argentine criollos were scattered across the countryside and it was like being transported to a different world compared to the city where they lived. You couldn't even see the blue sky in Recoleta unless you craned your head upward and peered through the tall buildings.

Many of the weekend mansions they passed in the country have an element of southern Spanish style in design and color, with angular foundations and high walls with stone molding trim, columned entries and clay tiled roofs, and painted a beautifully reflective white with mustard accent trim and forest green window sills. Marie spent time traveling through Andalusia three years ago, and she was dreaming of building a little country home in just the same style, only perhaps on a little horse farm near the mountains in Patagonia.

Nico had the travel details planned to the minute. They would reach their first stop at 9:20 to refuel with 60 liters of premium diesel at the station in Santa Rosa, which also had a cafe for coffee and breakfast pastries, and a clean restroom. Fifteen minutes should be plenty of time to fuel the car, gather food and drinks and handle any necessities. Another three and a half hours at 130 kilometers per hour and they would pass beyond the eastern marsh barrier into the great central pampas and gradually rise into the high desert mesa, and arrive at the Brazilian owned Petrobras station and restaurant at Cruce del Desierto at precisely 1:00 p.m.

If he was by himself he'd push on quickly, but Marie and the boy insisted on lunch inside and walking about for a few minutes admiring the flowering cactus, and God help him if they saw some stray dogs that needed a meal from the tourists. He increased his speed a little in anticipation.

Nico pulled into the Petrobras ahead of schedule and sent Marie and Cristian into the restaurant to get a table and order lunch.

"Get a table near the front, and order lunch while I

put fuel in the car, Marie. I don't want to waste any more time here than we have to," he ordered.

"Relax, Nico. Your precious trees will all still be there when we arrive," she said with a smirk and a grin.

He topped off the tank in the Mercedes, then pulled the car around to the front and backed into a good parking spot where he could keep an eye on it while they were eating. He didn't particularly trust these people in the campo any more than the ones in the city.

Nico and Marie shared a large bowl of pasta with bolognesa, fresh baked bread with some olive pesto from the groves in northern Mendoza province, and a bottle of white Torrontes wine from Salta. Cristian ordered a flattened and deep fried milanesa steak with french fries on the side. He only ate half of it, and the rest he saved and folded up in a paper napkin to give to the poor little dog he'd seen huddled by the front door. Cristian was always feeding the stray dogs everywhere he went, and he'd usually look at Marie and Nico and say, "I don't think he has a home. Do you think we should keep him?" The answer was always the same.

They settled into the car to start the last leg of the cross country drive to San Martin de Los Andes and pulled out onto the highway and turned due south. It was early afternoon in the early summer and hot in the desert, but in a couple of hours time they would arrive in the river valleys and forests of northern Patagonia with cooler temperatures and nice steady breezes from the Pacific. Marie didn't want to use the air conditioner, and rolled her window down halfway to fill the car with fresh air. She pulled her long hair into a ponytail to keep it under control in the wind, but it still whipped around the front of her face and her neck in the buffeting air inside the car.

Nico always started to feel just a little excited at this point in the trip every year, because soon he'd see the top of the mountains peering over the flat land to the west, and he'd think about the stories his father used to tell him about fishing in the mountains of Italy. He hadn't fished himself in several years because he was too busy working, but maybe this year he'd teach Cristian how to fish. Yes, this would definitely be the year he took time off to teach his son everything his father had taught him.

He glanced over at Marie and thought how beautiful she looked with her hair flitting around her face and her light summer dress dancing above her knees in the wind. Her shoes were off already, and her smooth legs stretched out to the front of the floorboard, and she let her head lay back against the shaped headrest and rolled her eyes to the left and smiled and stared into his eyes.

He was completely captivated by her. His life in the city was always so busy that he didn't often take the time to think about how deeply he loved this woman. But here in this place, far from the pressures and the noise of life and out on the open road, his mind would find a few moments of peace, and when it did, all he could think about was her.

"I'm sorry I was such an ass this morning," he said, as he stared back at her. "With everything going on in the city these days, I've been so afraid of something happening to you or Cristian that I just couldn't wait to leave. I keep having this feeling. A horrible feeling in the pit of my stomach, that something bad is coming."

"Nothing's going to happen, Nico. We're all together, and everything is going to be glorious this year in San Martin." Marie said with an assuring smile. "Just relax and enjoy the drive."

She reached over and lightly touched his forearm, then her hand glided down and clasped his. The warmth of her hand on his skin made his fears fade away, and released the clenched folds of skin across his forehead that never seemed to relax.

He couldn't imagine a life without her, and sometimes he couldn't understand how a woman like Marie had fallen in love with him. She was born to a wealthy and well connected family in Buenos Aires and she could have chosen from a thousand different eligible young men who were all part of the upper class in Argentina.

They met by chance one day at the grand botanical gardens in the center of the city where Nico was delivering a large order of custom outdoor furniture for the gardens, his first big commercial order for the family business, and Marie was spending an afternoon with a wealthy young suitor strolling along the pathways and admiring the plants and butterflies.

Nico remembered being physically stunned by her beauty, and almost unable to speak when she boldly approached him. She asked if she could sit on the hand carved bench he was placing between two native fuchsia trees, and all he could manage was a nod of his head as if he was paralyzed in her presence. She lowered herself slowly to the bench seat with back straight and head high, with her hands on her thighs to keep her skirt from sliding above her knees, and gracefully slid back onto the polished oak seat. Then her eyes lit up and she smiled.

"This is marvelous!" she said.

"Would you consider making one for my garden?"

"Yes. Yes I would love to make something for you," Nico said, in a crackling nervous voice.

And so went his first encounter with Marie d'Auvergne.

MARIE D'AUVERGNE WAS CHARACTERISTICALLY French slender, but not slender to the point of appearing frail or delicate. She had a light but strong frame, and athletic balance about her. Her hair was dark gleaming silk to the small of her back, and meticulously shaped into a shallow V at the base, which was the contemporary style for younger women of status in Buenos Aires social circles at the time. She wore it tastefully wound and wrapped when attending the opera or charitable events, but she preferred to let it hang to its length at parties and dinner gatherings.

Her eyes were her most commanding feature, and Nico often fell before them in willing servitude. They were large and well rounded, and symmetrically braced below fine thin brows the same color as her hair. At times they were a soft azure-gray like the Mediterranean Sea after a clearing storm, with pinpoint sparkles from rays of sunlight, that they shone a happiness and sense of hope when you gazed into them. At other times they were a steely-blue with focus and intent; or faded into the pale glacier blue that could drive a shiver through your spine without a word spoken or any visible sign of the anger that seethed inside her. And when she held her son in her arms they warmed and softened to the cast of the afternoon sky over the Andes.

She was elegant in repose, and alluring in motion, a moment rarely passed that others weren't admiring her. Her father, Jacques, was a worldly and well-traveled man. He was also wise enough to see the world changing around them, and the growing blend of cultures that was shaping the future of Argentina, so he insisted his daughters be submersed in foreign language and social environments.

Buenos Aires had private schools to match almost every major nation, and so every few years his daughters were uprooted from their boarding schools and placed in a completely new one. Three years in the British schools to learn English and the lifestyle of the Brits; then another in the French school, and a tour in the Italian.

It was nightmarish for young girls to be taken from the comfort of their friends and thrust into a new language and culture, but by the time Marie and her sisters were ready for university they each spoke four languages with native fluency, and could blend with almost any social circle with ease. She was groomed to become the perfect wife for a man of industry or influence, and her intellect made her a formidable adversary. Nico never had a prayer of besting her in an argument.

Despite her family's rich history and her classical education, she had a humor and wit that made her a fun companion on a long ride in the car and she adored the great open spaces and wild mountains of the Patagonian Andes. She looked forward to their annual trip through the countryside to the lakes region along the Chilean border, and even though it was long and tiring, she found something poetic or funny to say with every new vista and changing landscape along the journey.

She had a particular fascination for the wild creatures that they started seeing almost immediately after leaving the city, and she kept a secret little journal where she counted the numbers of foxes, eagles, condors and the ostrich-cousin Rheas, called *choiques* by the campesinos. She drew sketches of each to the best of her recollection with a little charcoal pencil, and gave them names to help her remember where she saw them. She loved the guanacos the best, with their always curious faces, large eyes and long lashes. They weren't as precious as their camelid cousins, the alpacas from the Peruvian Andes, but they were more handsome than the brutish llamas.

* * *

IT WAS late afternoon as they drove across the final high mesa and reached the twisting ribbon of two-lane blacktop that tacked back and forth down to the river valley below. The road signs warned once, twice, and even a third time to slow down and use caution because there was no shoulder to the road and the drop off to the down-mountain side in the corners wasn't protected by guardrails, and gravity was a bitch.

Making it even more challenging, was the unexpected and stunning view after they came around the first corner. After endless hours driving across a mind-numbing desert that was as flat as a pool table to the horizon, the eyes get easily startled by the dramatic landscape change and the colors, and the sheer drop in altitude rushing at you. Keeping your eyes on the road was hard, and made harder with a wife and son in the car gasping and squealing at the sudden view of emerald green water and trees and a roller coaster drop-off.

There were twenty seven sharp, slow-speed corners going down the mountain, and the elevation plummeted from 4400 feet above sea level to 2210 feet in a matter of minutes just riding the brakes down the road.

This was also a main travel route for cross country delivery trucks going back and forth to Chile, and logging trucks bringing fresh cut pine trunks stacked and tied on flat beds, and usually pulling doubles. The heavy laden trucks would creep down in low gear trying desperately to save their brakes, and the thundering "rap-rap-rap"_ of the engine braking could be heard for miles. If you got stuck behind one it was going to be a long slow trip down the mountain and the ultimate test of patience. Nico lost his patience on corner number sixteen.

Marie had come straight up in her seat and put on her fashionable polarized Gucci sunglasses to see the deep greens and blues in the Limay River through the late afternoon glare, and Cristian was squeezed up between the two front seats, and nearly sitting straddle of the hand brake to peer under the sun visors.

"Oh, there it is! Look Cristian, the Limay!" Marie said.

“Papa, the water is so green, I'll bet it's full of fish!" Cristian said to his father, but Nico was focused on the logging truck coming to a near full stop in front of him before beginning the descent.

Marie added, "I always feel like I'm almost home every time we reach here and see the river valley and the mountains. Look on the far side of the valley at the tall mountain, our property is just on the other side. Maybe we'll live there someday."

She and Cristian didn't mind at all that it was slow going behind the truck because they were mesmerized by the view and the longer it took, the better. Even though they drove through here every year, it never failed to excite them about the next few hours of beautiful scenery and wildlife.

Nico was calculating in his head every second of time he was losing in his planned arrival schedule, and growing more impatient with every corner they dragged around at less-than-walking speed behind the logging truck.

"Oh, for God's sake! Can't you go any faster!" he yelled at the truck in front out of frustration.

"I could get there faster by walking!"

He was inches away from the log truck's trailer rail, with the Mercedes in neutral and burning down the brake shoes when they cleared corner number sixteen. He rolled down his electric window to put his head out for a better view and eased to the left to peek around into the oncoming lane; it was clear.

"Finally!" Nico yelled.

He whipped the 300D to the left and shifted immediately into second gear and jammed the accelerator to the floor to pass, upshifting into third just as they roared past the nose of the truck and ripping like a bullet towards the next corner.

It didn't matter that he was behind the wheel of a

German luxury car, this was the style of driving that Italians were bred for. He stayed to the left side of the road to get the best line into the right-hand corner ahead, number seventeen; braked hard, downshifted back into second and dove to the inside of the blind corner.

When the french-made Michelin tires hit the light gravel that had washed onto the roadway after an evening rain, it was like driving on marbles. The front tires lost traction and pitched the front of the car directly at the drop-off on the outside of the corner and Nico spun the wheel frantically to the right, locking his arms in a cross-over and his thumbs twisted backwards in the steering wheel.

In a low guttural voice, Nico uttered, "Oh shit."

"Nico!" Marie shouted, then she was clenched.

The front end regained traction for an instant, but when the front tires grabbed the pavement, the momentum and downhill gravity threw the rear end of the car sideways and the shining champagne coach went into an unrecoverable death spin.

Cristian's small body was hurtled directly into the front windshield, head first. The safety glass frosted instantaneously, and glistened like a thickly woven spiderweb, covered with morning dew in the first rays of sunlight. He died quickly, and likely with no pain.

Marie had been so frightened by Nico's passing of the truck, that she was clutching the hand grip on the passenger door with her right hand, and pressing her palm against the dash with her left arm fully extended and elbow locked. The fear gripped her by the throat and strangled her vocal cords, and she couldn't utter a sound as the Mercedes flew sideways off the side of the mountain with her side going over first.

The sounds of screeching radials and grinding stones and gravel was replaced with a few moments of perfectly deadly silence, as the car tipped into the air and began a spinning roll, free of its weight against the earth. Nico was on the outside of the centrifugal spin and was ejected immediately through his open window.

He was fully aware in the midst of a surreal moment.

One second gripping the steering wheel, and the next suspended in the swirling dusty air in zero gravity. He didn't feel his body hitting the sandy patch of ground seconds later, or the outcropping of rock that arrested his fall and broke two of his short ribs and kept him from going off the steep cliff.

He looked up after hitting the ground, just in time to see the Mercedes crash back into the vertical rocky slope below, the side glass exploding in all directions, and spinning faster and faster to the bottom of the canyon, and Marie's long dark hair chaotically trying to escape the confines of the car through the window and float off into the wind.

There was no fire or explosion, because a diesel fueled engine doesn't usually produce fumes that ignite as easily as gasoline. There was only the piercing blackboard sounds of crushing German steel as it made impact with the rocks between its pirouettes to a final resting place on the high gravel bank above the river. Then a hissing, steamy gasp and clunk when the durable engine quit.

The driver of the log truck saw the brake lights flash, then the rear end of the silver Mercedes getting loose in the corner up ahead after going past him at a frightful speed, but he didn't see what happened after it rounded the turn and beyond his vision.

As he eased his way around the tight corner he could see scattered gravel and deep black tire tracks scorched into the pavement twirling together and back that resembled a sickeningly tarnished braided chain, and it vanished at the edge of the outer turn. He could still smell the bitter hint of burning rubber after the tires had been locked, and melted one side completely flat in the violent spin. He feared for the worse, but he looked ahead down the road and through the next corner below, to see if the Mercedes was speeding along farther down. It wasn't.

It took another mile and a half before the truck driver reached the flats below and pulled out in a special place for eighteen wheelers to stop and cool their brakes after the hill. Only then did he see the simmering wreckage laying directly in his line of sight to the east about 500 yards away. He looked up to where he thought the corner had been where the car flew off the road, and he could see a speck of a man crawling his way down the rocky mountain face.

The driver flagged down another passing car and pleaded for them to go directly to the police station in the nearest town up the highway, Piedra del Aguila (Eagle Rock), as soon as they could get there, but he knew an ambulance would be at least four hours away in this remote part of Patagonia, and looking at the wreckage and the drop the car had taken, he didn't think an ambulance would be much help anyway, except for the one person he could see crawling down the mountain.

"Tell them to expect dead bodies," he said.

An old Ford flatbed came along headed north from San Carlos de Bariloche with three provincial road crewmen, assigned to trim and burn the weeds along the route, and they pulled over and jumped out to help. When the truck driver pointed out the crushed silver lump on the hillside to the east, then pointed up to the corner where it leapt from the road, they grimaced. All three brought their fingers to their chest and made the sign of the cross in unison, and the older man with gray whiskers covering his face whispered under his breath, "Dios mio."

The road crewmen opened a rusty metal lockbox on the flatbed and pulled out a long heavy pry bar, a small medical kit that contained only a bottle of merthiolate and a few small adhesive bandages, and a neatly folded sheet of opaque plastic. Then the three of them scrambled along the rocky ledges and through the thorn bushes and chest high sage to reach the car.

The truck driver climbed across and upward directly to Nico, who was still barely half way down the mountainside. He reached him the same time as the crewmen reached the car, and he forced Nico to sit and catch his breath while he looked him over for injuries.

He was scratched and bloody on his face and had a deep gash down the length of his left forearm, but other than that he didn't see any obvious wounds. He thought it was possible he might be hurt inside, but he was definitely in shock and couldn't utter a word in response to any questions. Nico sat mute in the shale, and his eyes had the distant gaze of a man who's seen a thousand days of battle.

By the time Nico started regaining some of his senses, the road crewmen had pulled Marie and Cristian from the crumpled vehicle and laid them out on a smooth patch of fine river stone, side by side with their hands folded respectfully across their stomachs. He watched them from above as they shook the sheet of opaque plastic loose in the air and let it float down over the two bodies like a silk bed sheet.

Everything about his life; everything he had been, and everything he ever dreamed of doing, ended in that moment. He was as crushed beyond repair as the metal heap resting next to his wife and child.

The shock of how quickly his life was just devastated left only flashes of memory from the next several hours. People rushing and scurrying around him, car horns, yelling, the burning heat of the sun in his eyes, and being carried on a canvas stretcher to the roadside.

The first ambulance, a converted Ford pickup truck with a camper shell on the back, reached the scene and they set Nico on the tailgate and wrapped him in a blanket. The ambulance driver, who worked a regular job at the gas station, looked him over and cleaned the wound on his arm and taped it with gauze, but he couldn't get Nico to respond to any commands, so they knew they had to drive him up the highway to the nearest medical clinic in Piedra del Aguila as soon as the police released him.

The provincial police took charge of the scene and they tried to question Nico, but he stayed numb and silent. They took a statement from the truck driver and inspected everything thoroughly and photographed the scorch marks on the highway and the final resting place of the Mercedes, and the bodies of Marie and Cristian hidden beneath the plastic tarp, before they allowed the medical crews to remove the bodies and deliver them to the coroner's office in the provincial capital, Neuquen City.

A hundred or more cars inched their way past the scene. A lot of people rolled down their windows to get a better view but looked disappointed that they couldn't see anything but Nico sitting on the bumper wrapped in a blanket. Half of their day had been spent parked on the highway, and a glimpse of a really spectacular crash was the best they could hope for to salvage their wasted time. Many just sneered at him as they passed, feeling bothered and hungry, and bloated from holding their pee for the past three hours.

Their contempt passed unnoticed by Nico, as his suffering went unnoticed by the crowd.

He was adrift in the great void now. Encapsulated in a vacuum of time, utterly and completely alone. A place where the stream of minutes, hours, and days would flow around his shielded bubble of space without notice or reflection. Life continued in the stream, but within his private space it had ceased to function. Save for the rhythm of his clenching heart and slow, shallow breath, he was hovering between the flow of life, and the dark threshold of death.

Day Two

From his office window on the 5th floor, Jorge Rodriguez could see the sun setting between the skyscrapers of Buenos Aires and the traffic standing motionless in the afternoon rush below. He still had a few hours of work he wanted to finish up before he called it a night, and besides, he wouldn't be able to get anywhere on the highway right now anyway.

Jorge was a corporate lawyer. A savvy one. Trained in law through the public university, but his real education came in the streets and backrooms. He was a skilled deal maker and sharp as a razor.

His office was smartly decorated with plaques and certificates and awards from local organizations, and photographs of himself with important people. There was even one with the president of Argentina on a fishing trip in the Parana River north of Buenos Aires. He looked at that photo every day and thought about how far he had come, from growing up in a poor barrio on the edge of town, to being fishing buddies with the president.

Nico was along for that trip too, in fact, he was the one who took the photo of Jorge with the president smiling broadly and holding a huge golden dorado fish.

They'd been fishing together since they were boys, and Nico's father taught Jorge how to cast and gave him his first fly fishing rod as a birthday gift when he turned fifteen. Gerard used to take a couple days away from making furniture to take them by bus up to the El Tigre river and fish for sea trout and red drum fish that came in with the high tides, and they would make a fire and camp by the river, and he would tell the boys stories about the rivers and streams in Italy and France, and also sometimes tell them about making bamboo fly rods by hand. Gerard was a talented furniture maker, but the one thing he loved more, and was almost famous for at one time in his life, was crafting bamboo fly fishing rods.

Jorge and Nico hadn't done much fishing in the last few years because Nico was completely absorbed in growing his business after his father died. He was obsessed with it, and Jorge played a big role in the company.

Jorge was Nico's oldest and truest friend. He lived in the small house next door with his parents and eight brothers and sisters, when Gerard and Nico and his mother first came to start a new life in Buenos Aires.

He usually felt like Nico was his true brother and Nico's parents made him feel that way too. They had always wanted more children and Jorge sometimes felt a little lost in the crowd of his own family. He liked spending most of his time in the Azzarà house, and he took it upon himself to be Nico's personal tutor in Spanish and all things Argentine.

They were the same in many ways; intelligent, resourceful, and driven to succeed even as boys. But where Nico was serious and broody, Jorge was lighthearted and flowed through life like the ocean breeze in early spring. They both had ambitions to lift themselves and their families beyond the meager existence of the poor urban maze, but they approached it in completely different ways.

Nico saw opportunity and potential in his father's business and he used it to grind his way forward. He sacrificed, and investing his energy into growing and expanding, and acquiring more and more assets.

Jorge took advantage of the public education offered in Argentina, and became an attorney. He specialized in corporate law because he loved the art of the deal, meeting important people, and it gave him a chance to work with his best friend.

It was only natural that they ended up working together, Jorge handling all of Nico's business legal affairs and sitting on the board of his company, as they shared the same ideas and trusted each other with their very lives. Jorge stood next to Nico as his best man when he was married to Marie, and he proudly accepted the honor of being named as Cristian's legal godfather at his baptism.

It was 5:30 in the afternoon when the call came in from Marie's father, Jacques d'Auvergne.

"Jorge, have you heard from Nico?"

"No señor, Nico and Marie and Cristian left early this morning to drive to San Martin de los Andes. Nico needed to do the summer inspection and accounting at the timber estancia."

"Th ... they're dead, Jorge. My Marie and Cristian, they're dead." Jacques's voice choked, and he took a deep breath before he continued. "The provincial police in Neuquen called an hour ago to tell us they were killed in a crash somewhere along the highway in the province. They couldn't tell me anything about Nico, only that he was taken by ambulance to Piedra del Aguila. I'm chartering a plane to fly us to Neuquen City later tonight."

Jorge fell forward onto his mahogany desk with his face in his left hand, and his right hand loosely holding the phone. His stomach wrenched and all he could hear for a few moments was own heartbeat thundering in his ears.

"Señor d'Auvergne, this can't be. It just can't be."

Jacques didn't answer.

"Señor, I will gather some things and meet you at the airport."

He met Jacques d'Auvergne at the regional airport

later that night, and they looked at each other with numb, swollen eyes but said nothing. It was a two hour flight to the town of Neuquen in the western province of Argentina, in the northern most region of Patagonia, and it passed in complete silence, save for the roar of the engines.

They flew in a Piper Twin Comanche, a small twin engined aircraft that could carry six passengers, but on this flight there were only two. Jacques took his place in the front row on the starboard side and stared blankly at the instrument panel over the pilot's shoulder, neither understanding, nor caring about the complex array of gauges and dials and buttons. He was secretly hoping that the flight would never end, because he didn't want to face the reality of what lay ahead.

Jorge sat one row back and to the left, and gazed through the small portal at the star-filled southwestern sky that lay over the Andes mountains, inching closer with every hum and bump of the twin props. It was the time of the annual summer meteor showers that blaze across the southern hemisphere, and from time to time, a glowing green ball of light would streak through the darkness, then flicker out as it fell to some unknown destination in the Andean range. He wondered, for just an instant, if they were lighting the way to where he would find his best friend.

They arrived at the small regional airport, and took a taxi to the provincial police headquarters to meet with investigators. Then Jacques was taken to the morgue to identify and claim the bodies of his daughter and grandson, and have them flown back to Buenos Aires.

Jorge rented a car in Neuquen as soon as the rental company opened at 7:00, and made the three hour drive to Piedra del Aguila, and he asked the first local he saw walking on the street as he entered the small town where the medical clinic was, and drove straight to it. There was only a nurse on duty, and the doctor had left to treat an older woman who couldn't leave her house a few blocks away.

The nurse told Jorge that Nico had been brought in by ambulance yesterday afternoon, and they treated his cuts and bruises, and they thought he may have a broken rib or two. They sent for another vehicle to transport him to a bigger hospital in Neuquen that had X-ray machines, but when it arrived, Nico had vanished. No one saw him leave, and they had no idea where he went. The police came to check on him later, and they looked all over town but didn't find a trace of him.

"Do you know where the accident happened?" Jorge asked.

"The ambulance driver works a regular job at the gas station on the main avenue, maybe he can tell you exactly where it was." The nurse told him.

Jorge found the local ambulance driver and medical tech at the Petrobras on main street, and he told him the accident scene was about one hour driving time away with light traffic, and easy to find.

"Look for the black tire marks in a curve about

halfway down the mountain. That's where the Mercedes went over, but it's at the very bottom now down by the river bank. What is left of it," he said. "I never saw anything like it. I mean, a guy walking away from a crash like that." He continued. "Angels must have been holding his hands when he flew out of that car."

Jorge thought if Nico had gone to look for Marie and Cristian in Neuquen, then he would have run into him somewhere between the police station or the hospital, but something in the back of his mind was telling him to go to the river.

He went inside and filled his thermos with hot water, to make traditional yerba mate tea on the trip. He bought a small folding map of the provincial roads, even though there were only a few roads that largely ran north or south, then he filled his rental car with fuel anticipating that he may have to drive many miles in search of Nico. There were no other gas stations between here and San Martin de Los Andes.

He started his drive south towards the Limay not with a sense of hope, but with a sense of dread.

Fifteen Hours Earlier

Nico looked around the small clinic with only two beds other than the one he was laying on, and a shiny metal rolling table with a few instruments on it next to him. His mind was replaying the accident over and over again like a horror movie scene that endlessly haunts your sleep. The slide and wheel lock. Screeching tires and flying stones, and floating weightless in the air. He couldn't really remember seeing anything happen after the truck driver showed up and made him sit in the rocks while he looked him over. It was a giant gap in his recollection.

"I have to get back there now," he said to himself.

"They'll be coming back and wonder where I am."

He was confused and frightened, and the pain medicine the doctor gave him for his broken ribs were clouding his thoughts.

"If I leave now I can be there before dark, and I'll be there waiting for them when they come back," he thought.

Nico gathered himself up and slid off the folding bed, put his shirt back on, and walked straight out the front door of the clinic. The doctor had left for the evening, thinking nothing else would need to be done with this patient, and the nurse had just gone next door to borrow some sugar for her late day tea.

No one saw Nico as he walked to the main road and flagged down the first passing pickup truck and asked for a ride. The driver seemed a little confused when Nico told him to stop at the bottom of the long series of spiraling corners down from the mountain, but Nico told him, "I have to meet my wife and son here. They'll be along any minute." The driver nodded his head and left him standing in the dusty roadside.

Nico stood by the road and looked out over the river for a long time, like he couldn't really remember why he was here; then he saw the crumpled remains of the Mercedes on the river bank to the east, and the horror movie in his head started rolling again.

The world spinning, the sounds of crashing metal and falling rock, and the deafening silence when it ended. He could see himself crawling down the rock face and sliding through the loose shale and felt the thorn bushes tearing at his shirt. He looked down at his arm and saw the shirt torn and bloody, and realized this wasn't a bad dream. And now he remembered seeing Marie and Cristian being pulled from the wreckage and laid out on the river bank.

His mind was flashing forward and back. One instant knowing they were gone, and the next expecting to see them coming up the trail.

He walked across the hills from the highway to where he'd seen them last, laying on the river stone by the Mercedes, and collapsed to the ground. A sickle moon was rising in the evening sky from the direction of Buenos Aires, and it cast a faint buttery glow along the water, and the few parts of his car that were unmarred by the tumble, and Nico could see his own distorted reflection in the bent metal. He sat there motionless, unable to speak, or cry, or think. His body felt paralyzed and all he could hear was a high pitched ringing in his ears as the sun fell below the mountain tops.

A light misty rain started falling, and the light from the moon faded into pitch darkness. For a while, Nico didn't notice the damp or lack of light. But then the faint tapping sound of the rain falling on plastic caught his attention. He reached his hand out in front of him into the blackness and swept it across the desert sand until he felt it. It was the plastic tarp the road crewmen had draped over the bodies of Marie and Cristian, now rolled into a crumbled ball and caught in a thorny bush.

He pulled it free from the thorns and into his lap, and it crackled and squeaked as he slowly turned it over and around in his hands and he could see it in his mind, outlining the shape of Marie's most feminine features. Her delicate nose, her full lips and firm chin, her breasts and petite little feet as it covered her lifeless figure on the ground.

He unfolded it, and pulled it around himself and over his head to shield off the raindrops. The light 'tap-tap-tap' around his head brought a vision of Marie, lightly rapping her perfectly manicured fingernails on the polished hardwood dash of the Mercedes. "What are we waiting for?" She said. Then she laughed at him. She always laughed. Even when Nico was impatient, or angry; she laughed. And her laughter disarmed him.

He smiled at the thought of her, and suddenly he could smell a remnant of her french perfume on the inside of the plastic tarp where it had made a sticky connection with the moist skin of her throat. He pulled it tighter around his face and breathed as deeply as he could to capture every last molecule of her, and he could feel her warm breath on his neck.

"Marie," he said, "Can you remember the last time we did this? It was over ten years ago, when I came to buy the timberland, and you came along with me because you were desperate to see Patagonia."

"Yes, my love," she whispered into his ear.

"We sat outside in the green summer grass that first night, drinking wine from paper cups and gazing at the stars. We'd never seen stars like that in Buenos Aires. They filled the sky."

It was on that night years ago, as they lay under the open starlit sky, wrapped together in a soft woven alpaca wool blanket, that they made love and brought new life to the world. Cristian was conceived that night, here in the wilds of Patagonia under a blanket with the Southern Cross slowly drifting overhead.

"Why didn't we do this more often?" he said to her. But she didn't answer.

The perfume pulled him back to the world, and he glanced upward from under the tarp but there were no stars shining tonight. There was nothing but empty cold blackness and the constant tapping of rainfall. And yet, there was that last fleeting trace of Marie's wonderful scent. She was still with him, he thought, giving him one last embrace beneath this shitty piece of plastic under the dark desert sky.

By midnight the light tapping rainfall had grown into a torrential downpour driven by fierce winds coming from the Pacific and howling off the lee side of the Andes mountains, and he was clinging to the plastic as it flapped in the wind like a sheet hung out in a hurricane. The rain drops were stinging his face and arms, and as numb as his conscious mind was, his subconscious knew he'd be dead by morning if he didn't find shelter. The only option he had was the car.

Nico crawled into the back seat of the crushed Mercedes through the contorted window opening and laid across the rich dark leather seat, squeezing himself into the space with only an inch or two between his head and the flattened roof.

The rain pouring down sounded like a metallic symphony over his head, but he was strangely comfortable wedged into the confinement. He'd never even sat in the backseat of his Mercedes before. "How many people actually even know what their backseat feels like?" He thought. Cristian was the only one who ever sat back here.

"This feels good," he thought. "Cristian is here with me."

Cristian's school backpack was firmly wedged into the floorboard between the front and rear seats, and he could smell the pungent aroma of the dirty socks that he pulled off his little feet after the lunch stop in Cruce del Desierto, blended with the new-car smell coming from the waxed leather seat his head was resting on. He sense of smell was powerful right now. Stronger than all of his other senses. Focused like a razor.

His eyes were useless in the pitch black, and his body and fingertips were numb, so the world around him was being displayed completely through smell. Marie's perfume had been the trigger. Then the rain began to fall in great waves that struck like a hammer against the roof of the car and his hearing came alive again.

The constant pounding above him was deafening, and it transported him back in time to his childhood, and the desperate journey he made with his father and mother to reach the safety of Argentina when he was about the same age as Cristian.

BY THE FINAL years of the second great war in Europe there was little call for his father's furniture maker skills. The shop where he worked closed after the first year of fighting, and Gerard struggled to keep his family alive and safe from the ravages of war.

Not long after the war ended, a priest in their local church arranged for him to work for fares for the three of them on a cargo ship bound for South America, and he leapt to a new life. They bundled a handful of meager possessions into a single canvas bag and traveled through the night to the port town of Genoa, then boarded the rusting hulk of a ship in the dead of night.

The sea voyage was long and weary in rough Atlantic current and early summer storms raging west from the

Ivory Coast. For twenty one days and nights the three of them were damp, dirty and almost always on the verge of puking. They slept stacked together in a single berth, and endured the endless metallic pounding of the diesel engines turning huge twin screws in the hull below. Smashed into the backseat of the Mercedes with the rain beating on the roof felt eerily familiar, and welled deep inside him the same fear of not knowing what tomorrow will bring, or if there will even be a tomorrow.

His father Gerard started over with almost nothing after arriving in Buenos Aires. He worked in a small rented shop in a back ally, with only a rusty throwaway hand saw, gifted to him by the ship engineer, and two carving chisels he smuggled into his bag from the shop where he used to work in Turin.

He made functional and affordable chairs and tables, and eventually made furniture for some of the wealthier people that left Italy and France and Switzerland on the more expensive luxury ships to start over in Buenos Aires after the war. There were even a few German speaking customers that Gerard suspected were former nazis, smuggled out of Genoa before the fall of the Third Reich. He didn't care who they used to be; they paid him well for good work.

* * *

WHEN NICO DID FINALLY fall into a sleep-like state, he

saw images of Cristian running through his head like a stuttering 8mm movie reel. He saw a nurse placing a baby bundled in a celeste blue blanket into his arms. Then a diaper-bound toddler making a waddling run to him from Marie's arms across the kitchen floor.

He saw Cristian as a five year old, running into the house on a Saturday morning with bloody baby teeth dangling loose from his mouth after a fall on his bicycle; and he saw him cheering in front of the television for his favorite Argentine soccer star, Mario Kempes, during the World Cup.

And the last image he saw, the one that wouldn't leave him for the remainder of that rainy night, was a blurry vision of Cristian lurching forward; then the windshield of the car turning to a smoky frost.

There were no voices or sounds in his images, only the constant beat of the rain striking metal only inches from his ears, and neither the rain nor the images would cease until the sun rose on a new day.

* * *

AS HE ROUNDED the final bend of the road on the upper flat mesa, Jorge could see the far desert horizon suddenly drop away from the sky as the deep river valley opened ahead of him, and it gave him the same impending rollercoaster-drop sensation that made Marie and Cristian's eyes widen the day before.

He navigated slowly down the serpentine roadway

looking for the telltale tire marks the ambulance driver had warned him about, and he saw them distinctly carved into the tarmac halfway down the mountain; but where they seemed to disappear from the road there was nothing but cliff and thousands of feet of air.

It scared the shit out him just slowing down to peek over the edge. "Oh my god, Nico. The ambulance driver was right, an angel had to be looking after you," he whispered to himself.

Ten corners farther down the road and he reached the valley floor and the pullout, and he parked his rental car along side the road and stepped out not knowing what he might find. And also afraid of what he might find.

He looked back up the mountain to see where the car had fallen, and he could see the scouring impact trail of the Mercedes as it ricocheted down to the bottom. There he saw the crumpled ball of steel that no longer resembled an automobile, and again, he shook his head as if it couldn't have really happened and whispered, "Oh my god, Nico."

There were no obvious signs of Nico anywhere, only a worn trail through the brush out to the wreck from the road crews and rescuers and police migrating back and forth from the highway, but nothing else. He had secretly hoped he might find Nico walking by the roadside, but knowing that he disappeared from the clinic in Piedra del Aguila the night before and that he had injuries and he wasn't responding to anyone, he now had to consider that Nico might be laying dead somewhere in the desert.

Everything was still damp from a heavy rainfall last night, and being in shock and exposed to the cold night air and rain could kill a healthy man, let alone one who was injured. Then he saw the birds flush in the distance from around the wreckage. He couldn't tell what they were from that far, and he didn't really know about birds anyway, but they might have been vultures or maybe even condors.

The only thing he knew about birds like these, is that they were harbingers of death. Black as night and big enough that he could see them from so far away. Something had spooked them into flight.

Jorge stepped off the road into the sandy path and started picking his way through the brush and thorny michay bushes. It took him twenty minutes to reach the place where the desert scrub opened into the upper waterline of the bank, and the level bed of river stone where the car came to its final resting place, and as he pulled free of the last clawing thorns he looked at his shredded clothes. He was still wearing the grey suit he'd been in when he received the call from Jacques back in Buenos Aires.

"Great. Trashed my best suit," he said to himself. His pants were fairly shredded, and his white Armani dress shirt was speckled with holes and thread pulls and spots of his own blood seeping through, and his leather dress shoes were scratched and full of sand and stones.

He realized how stupid he looked standing there in the middle of the bush in lawyer clothes, with a fancy leather mate case draped over his shoulder like he was going to meet a friend in the central city park.

Then he heard movement from inside the car, and the squeaking sound of a leather cushion as someone or something wriggled in the confinement of the back seat. He approached the car cautiously and kneeled down to peer through the window, and saw Nico's dirt encrusted face staring back at him.

It was one of those moments when you feel a tremendous sense of relief like a heaviness has just fallen away from you, then in the same instant, you realize there's a new pain coming. Jorge had been in a state of disbelief since yesterday afternoon and all through the night traveling with Jacques until he saw photographs of the accident scene and the bodies of Marie and Cristian. Then it turned to fear and dread, not knowing what happened to Nico.

Now he knew Nico was alive, but the eyes staring back at him were completely void of emotion or recognition. He was looking at the empty shell of a man who had once been so full of energy and passion. So he did what he'd always done when things got tough in his life; he pulled his chin up, and smiled.

"There you are. I've been looking all over for you," he said. "Please come out and sit with me, Nico."

He reached his hand forward through the window

and gently clasped Nico's blood caked hand, but felt little strength gripping him back.

"Come on, it's ok."

He beckoned him with a light wave of his left hand and a compassionate smile like he might have made for a terrified stray dog that was huddling back in the safety of a dark place. Nico inched forward to squeeze through the opening and Jorge pulled him free. Then they sat down next to the car.

Jorge spent all night and half the day thinking about what to say to Nico and what to do when he found him, but nothing he said could change what had happened, and nothing would comfort Nico. They sat for hours in silence there in the gravel together, Nico in his soiled and bloody clothes unchanged for two days now, and Jorge in torn slacks and a ruined Armani shirt with the sleeves rolled halfway up the forearm, and his city-whitened skin starting to redden in the afternoon heat.

"Let's have some mate," Jorge blurted out. It was idiotic, but it was all he could think of to say, and the silence was suffocating him.

He opened the crafted leather case he'd carried with him from the road, and pulled out a thermos of hot water from the station in Piedra del Aguila, a small bag of imported and finely ground yerba mate, and a dark woody polished gourd cup with silver trim.

The trimming on the gourd, and the ornate sterling silver straw, called a *bombilla,* were hand crafted art work. Nico had one just like it, as they were gifts given to both of them by a wealthy client. But sitting here in the gravel, both of them torn and bloodied and mentally wasted, the social implications of the gourd was meaningless. It was just one man trying to connect with his friend in the most Argentine way he could think of.

He mixed the mate with a little sugar in the gourd, then slowly poured hot water into the center until it bubbled up to the surface. He let it rest for a few moments to start seeping, then extended it out to his friend for the first sip. Nico's eyes were open but his mind was far away, and he neither saw nor responded to his friend's gesture.

"Ok then, I'll take the first," Jorge said.

He looked away at the river and sipped at the mate in quiet thought, and when he started getting close to the bottom he opened up the thermos and refilled it again, and offered it back to Nico without a word. Nico's gaze never changed, but probably just out of reflex, his blood caked left hand came forward and accepted the gourd, then slowly moved it up so his dried lips could wrap lightly around the bombilla and he took a slow deep pull from the bitter-sweet liquid.

For just an instant, he blinked and his eyes shifted downward, before returning to his far-off gaze. Then the gourd and his hand eased down like it was fighting a tremendous weight of gravity and came to rest on his thigh.

Jorge saw the blink and thought to himself, "It's a

good sign, my friend is still in there somewhere."

"Nico, you should come with me now. Let me take you to the hospital so the doctors can care for you. You're injured, and you also need to eat."

"No. I won't leave them!" Nico lashed in anger. "They're here! I could feel her here with me last night, and I know she's here." Then he stood and took a few steps over to the place where their bodies had lain the last time he saw them, and sat back down facing the river.

He turned from stoic to violent in a millisecond. His mind was retreating into a deep, dark recess away from the physical plane; as far away as it could go, and as fast as it could get there. Any attempts at rational thought were wasted on him, and maybe dangerous.

"Shit," Jorge thought to himself. "He'll stay here and die if I let him."

Jorge had to think fast. If he tried to be forceful with Nico, it wasn't going to end well for either one of them. But he had to keep Nico alive until he came to his senses; then he could get him to a hospital. But he had nothing with him. No food, no clothes, nothing that might keep them both from freezing to death or starving. All he thought to bring was a damn mate thermos.

For a moment, he considered the idea of going to the nearest town and getting the Gendarmerie to come and drag him out in a straight jacket and take him to the hospital in Neuquen. But then he thought to himself, "If I do that, Nico will hate my guts for the rest of his life. He'll never forgive me." So he quickly dismissed it.

There was only one thing he could do. He had to leave Nico here and make a run to the nearest big town, San Martin de Los Andes, to buy supplies and get back here before Nico died. It would take one or two days to make the turnaround, but at least Nico had been smart enough to crawl into the back seat of the car to get out of the rain last night, and there was water to drink from the river.

It was a gamble he had to take.

"Ok, ok. I understand, Nico," he said, trying to diffuse Nico's anger. "You can stay here as long as you need to. I'm going to drive to San Martin de Los Andes and get some food and supplies, and we'll stay." Jorge said. "I'll call everyone back in Buenos Aires and let them know I found you and that you're staying here for a while. I'll talk to the police, then I'll be back here in a day. Drink some water from the river when you need it, and get back in the car if it starts raining again."

Nico faintly nodded his head, but never took his gaze from the river, and Jorge came over and put his hand on his shoulder, "Nico, we'll get through this. Just stay alive." Then without saying another word he turned in a deliberate march to his car parked on the highway.

It was nearly 10:00 p.m. before the light failed at this southern latitude in the summer months, and again it brought threatening rain clouds from the Pacific

Ocean and the drops falling on the rocks and plants could be heard slowly coming like footsteps inching closer in the darkness. Nico gathered up his plastic tarp and crawled to the safety of the backseat in the Mercedes and wedged the tarp across the opening. He curled tightly into a ball to stay warm, and the smashed down headliner formed a life saving cocoon from the outside world.

He eventually drifted off to sleep to the sound of the rain pounding the roof over his head, but he had fitful dreams. Dreams of a boy standing by the river and staring across the water as if he were looking for something he'd lost. In the dream, Nico tried to walk closer to the boy but he could never close the distance, and if he tried to see the boy's face it was always shadowed from the brilliant moonlight.

Only one time did the boy turn back to look at Nico, but he still couldn't see his features, and the boy raised his arm and pointed across the raging river to the calm water under the willows, and an enormous dark shape rolled to the surface and violently thrashed the water sending spiraling waves against the shoreline.

It was a gigantic fish with eyes as black and evil as a demon from hell, and it was calling to the boy and beckoning him into the water to devour him. Nico called to the boy and begged him to stay away from the water. He could tell the boy knew nothing about the ways of the river and the creatures that lived there, and this one would be his doom.

Day Three

❧

Nico woke to the sound of his own voice, pleading to a spirit to stay away from the river, and he was still shrouded in darkness with only a sliver of dust-speckled sunlight beaming down in front of his face through the narrow opening of the car window. The rain had stopped, and he could hear the calls of river birds wading along the shore in gossiping flocks.

He could hear the sound of water rolling and breaking around the smooth face of boulders, and from inside the remains of the car it echoed in thundering waves. He wriggled his way out feet first through the window and tried to stand up and stretch, but he was aching and stiff, and just now realized that his sides hurt like hell from two cracked ribs. He could barely take a breath without a searing pain around his abdomen.

It was a clear, cool summer morning and the river was running at full power from the steady snow melt.

He could see trout rising along the edge of an eddy that circled back on itself, as the river moved around a huge boulder in the center. And on the opposite side of the river there were willow trees that lined the banks with long green strands draping down to the water and swaying lightly in the breeze. A few fish were rolling in the shade below, sipping insects as they fell from the trees with each little gust of wind.

Nico hadn't fished in many years, since before his father died, and couldn't remember the last time he stopped for just a few minutes to admire the river. His father, Gerard, taught him to read the river when he was very young. Much younger than Cristian. He taught him to see the way the current moved and created channels and eddies, and soft pockets where the fish liked to rest and wait for food to pass by. He taught him about the life of the little insects as they hatch from eggs buried in the sandy bottom of the river, then they float up during the day and change into other little flying creatures that spring out of their shells when they reach the surface of the water. "Learn how the river lives," he said, "and you will never be hungry a day in your life."

Nico promised Cristian he would teach him to fly fish this year here in Patagonia, if he had time. He promised him the same thing the year before, and the year before that year.

"I've been telling him that for the last three years," he thought to himself.

"This would have been a good place. Open space, with no trees or bushes behind to tangle his line while he was learning to cast the rod. An easy shallow bank to wade in to the water and make short casts to where trout are feeding." Then suddenly he said, "This is perfect, I'll teach him here."

His mind had shifted again, away from the world we know to a place where the spirits live. And Cristian stood there by his side. "Let's go son," he said. He crept slowly to the edge of the water, to keep from spooking a nice rainbow trout that was sipping morning mayflies in a foamy line along the current close to the bank. "Can you see him holding behind that little rock, and then he pops up to take a fly as it gets close?" he said to Cristian. "He's saving his energy by resting, and letting his breakfast come to him." Cristian smiled and nodded his head.

"Now make a nice easy cast up ahead so your fly lands in that foamy line coming down the river, and let it drift right down to him." He was standing behind Cristian in his mind, lightly gripping his hand with the rod and helping him make a smooth cast, the two of them moving as one.

"A couple of easy strokes to pull out some line, then stop your rod tip high out front, so the line will unfold in the air and float down to the water."

Nico spent the next hour in a waking dream. Standing by the river's edge with Cristian casting and laughing, and reciting all of the things his father had taught him as a boy when he fished for the first time.

"BUEN DÍA, SEÑOR." Called a voice behind him.

Nico snapped awake from his day dream with Cristian when he realized he wasn't alone on the river bank. Above him on the rocky ledge was a towering figure, backlit by the burning morning sun. He looked like a giant until Nico tilted his head and held his hand above his right eye to shield the glare. Instead of a giant, it was a small but stout looking gaucho mounted atop a beautifully speckled grey criollo horse. Nico acknowledged him with a simple tilt of his head, but spoken words were still slow to slip from his mouth.

The gaucho reached up and respectfully pulled the boina hat from his head. "Forgive me for disturbing you," he said.

He knew exactly who Nico was, and how he came to be here on this river bank because news of tragedy travels fast in this land, but among the gaucho culture they see no reason to reflect with more words on things that are obvious. He offered only his name as a polite introduction, "I'm called Pablo."

Nico responded almost autonomously, "I am Nicholas Azzarà."

"Mucho gusto, Don Nicholas." Pablo responded, with his most formally respectful greeting, and using the "Don" prefix to acknowledge Nico's social class. It's rarely used in Argentina anymore, but he was trying to be particularly polite by using the old Castilian, given the circumstances.

Pablito, as his family and friends called him, glanced at the crushed Mercedes, but said nothing. In his mind, he was considering how many spirits must be surrounding and protecting this man, because the car looked like a Quilmes beer can, guzzled and then smashed with the heel of a boot.

The tale of the accident had worked its way among the locals and road crews and reached him the day before. This stretch of rolling desert mesa along the Limay and into the next valley to the west was but a small section of a very large private estancia, and it was Pablito's responsibility to care for this section of land and the horses, cattle and wildlife on it, and occasionally defend it from poachers and interlopers.

He saddled up in the early morning before the rising sun and made his way across the ridge and along the shoreline to come see the car wreckage to make sure it wasn't a danger to the property or animals, and to report back to his administrator on what was happening with the man rumored to be squatting at the site.

From a distance, he'd been watching Nico for some time while his horse carefully navigated the rocky trail down the ridge, then along the upper seasonal water line of the river where uprooted trees and debris formed little bulkheads. What he saw confused him, and made him reevaluate his original intentions.

He came here with the idea that he might have to forcefully drive someone away from this land, at the point of a knife or a gun if need be. He had driven away poachers, squatters and campers from this area before, because it was so easy to reach from the highway, and they could poach fish, or kill deer or livestock and have them loaded and be gone quickly. But this man wasn't behaving like a poacher, this was something he had never seen before.

"This man isn't squatting or poaching, he's just gone mad," he said to himself, while he watched him swaying back and forth in a rhythmic motion, and then laughing and smiling and talking to some phantom that only he could see.

Pablo kept looking farther upstream and down, and into the bushes on the higher shoreline, thinking there must be some other person that he couldn't see with whom the man was having an interesting chat. He didn't want to ride into an ambush of three or four armed men and be shot in the back.

But as he watched the scene unfolding before him with a careful eye, as would a working gaucho who sees more than the average person from the city would, he saw more. Much more. The water and wind moved precisely as the man moved, whether it was perfect timing on the part of the man, or the man was commanding them he couldn't tell. He wasn't a man standing in a river; he was like a living part of the river. The fish were rising and splashing the surface almost in unison with the man's motion, as if he were instructing them when and where to feed.

He thought to himself, "Maybe he's not mad at all. Maybe God is speaking to him in a different way now." The idea frightened him a little.

He remembered an ancient looking Mapuche woman many years ago telling him that the great Creator of All Things sometimes tries to speak to humans now through the animals, and trees and the Earth, because men have long ago forgotten how to hear his voice directly. Even now we're still mostly ignorant, as his faithful messengers are trying to communicate all around us.

Then something else occurred to him. Perhaps this man, who had nearly died two days ago in a car crash that killed his entire family, and who has obviously been here without any way to care for himself, is just starving. He's so hungry he's lost his mind, and he thinks he actually has one of those store bought fishing canes in his hands.

"Maybe if I get him some breakfast he'll get his strength back and his mind right, and then he'll leave on his own," he thought.

Pablo had never used an actual fishing rod in his life, and only seen a couple up close. They looked complicated, and difficult, but sometimes he watched visiting fly fishermen from a distance as he rode the hills on horseback, and the rods twisting and flexing, and lines tracing elegant loops forward and back through the air and reaching incredible distances across the water looked as magical as anything he had seen.

He may never have used a real fishing rod, but his knowledge of the river and all the creatures that lived in the water still made him a skilled fisherman. He used a simple device that's seen all over Argentina in the hands of people who fish for food rather than just for art or pleasure; an old coffee can, wrapped with discarded fishing line salvaged from the river banks during the low season.

The city fishermen who came here in the warm months always left a treasure of fishing line and flies and lures and hooks tangled in the trees and bushes. He would wrap the line around the coffee can, leave five or six feet off to spin in circles to gather momentum, and launch it like David's sling to his chosen spot in the river. The line peeled as smartly off the can as a modern day spinning reel that city people pay a week's wages for. He could retrieve it, rewind it, and launch it again nearly as fast as a real fishing rod equipped fisherman. He came home with fish to feed his family dinner on a regular basis.

Pablito swung his right leg over the rump of the horse and eased himself to the ground. He tied his horse's reins to a stump, then reached into a woven wool bag that was hanging from his saddle loop and pulled out his shiny tin coffee can wrapped tightly with mylar fishing line. He made only a fleeting eye contact with Nico as he walked to the river, passing by the place

Nico had been "fishing" with Cristian, and moved a bit upstream until he found a spot close enough that he could reach the willows on the far bank without having to wade in his leather boots.

He spun off a length of line, reached into his vest pocket and pulled out a fresh black *tabano.* They're nasty little biting flies that come out this time of year and make life a misery for men and animals, but if you swat a few and keep them in your pocket, you'll always have something the trout will bite. He threaded the gooey remains of the fly onto the little rusty hook, then made a few swings with the line and let it sail to the other side of the river. A moment later he was pulling the line hand over hand with a nice little trout in tow.

Within a few minutes he reeled in a second fish. Then he pulled his knife from a scabbard in the small of his back, and gutted them both there in the river, sending their entrails to the pancora crabs and washing their bodies out in the clean mountain water.

He'd left early this morning with nothing but a mate in his stomach, and thought a trout breakfast would be fine right now as well, and it would certainly be good for this poor man who was touched in the head. He walked back up to the clearing in the gravel near the Mercedes and lit a small fire with twigs and dried sage brush and stacked a few river rocks around the windward side to keep it from blowing away, and laid his fishing gear and match box down beside him on the rocks.

Nico stood in silence and stared to the east across

the flat mesa that points back to Buenos Aires, and said nothing nor made any movement while the little gaucho cooked the two fish over a low glowing fire. When they were lightly crisp on each side, Pablito pulled one from over the flame and blew on it for a moment to cool it to the touch, then lifted the flakes of pink flesh away from the skin with the tip of his knife and ate them at a very leisurely pace.

Again, he saw no reason to tell Nico that the other trout belonged to him, because it was an obvious matter. He figured this man who had to be hungry by now would eat or not at his will, and Pablito had done the charitable thing to catch and prepare the meal.

When he was done, Pablito stood and stretched his back muscles, and without a word he untied his horse and lead him around to a large stone to give his short legs a little advantage to reach the stirrup, and in one smooth motion pulled himself atop the tall sheepskin layered saddle.

Gauchos walk and talk like mortal men when they're on the ground, but as soon as they mount a horse they become something else. It's as if they've moved into an ethereal realm that was meant only for them. He looked like a creature of the water that had been creeping around uncomfortably on the rocks, then returned to the safety of the river, and transformed into a graceful, gliding elemental. All men probably have something they were born to be; but only a fortunate few find their given place in the world.

He knew that Nico would leave this sad place of death very soon and return to Buenos Aires, or die from exposure and starvation, so he didn't need to mention that he was on private property, it was obvious. He hoped it wouldn't be the latter because he didn't want to have to deal with another dead body in his puesto, and the Policia with their endless paperwork and questions, and more visits from the property administrator, who could be difficult, but his livelihood depended on him being respectful and following his commands.

"I must check this part of the estancia every so often, so I will see you again very soon," Pablito said. Then he pulled the reins and sharply spun his horse to the north and headed off along the rocky river trail in a rolling cantor.

Nico was still staring to the eastern horizon, and he turned his head and nodded, but avoided any direct eye contact. He glanced up again as Pablito prodded his horse with a heel, then at the little fish hanging over the coals; but only a small part of him was really aware of the physical world, and that part felt neither hunger nor fear or emotion of any kind. The most of him was drifting in some other place and time.

Day Four

Four days had passed since the accident, and the driver of the logging truck came back from delivering his load of pine to the northern city of Cordoba by the same route on his return trip to Chile. When he came through Piedra del Aguila, he asked the locals what became of the poor man in the Mercedes, and they relayed all that they knew, which was very little, only that he had disappeared. A bus driver passing through from the south had mentioned that he saw someone at the crash site the day before, so perhaps the man was still there by the car.

The truck driver went to the local hardware store and bought a few items before leaving. When he reached the turnout at the bottom of the twisting hill, he stopped and carefully built a traditional little shrine, about a foot high, made of stacked stones adhered with a little mortar. It had three sides and an angled roof, and was open to the front so passing travelers could stop and place an offering of water or food inside, or just light a candle to a saint.

He built it on the edge of the road where Nico had sat on the tailgate of the ambulance and watched the bodies of his wife and son being taken away. When he finished, he lit a candle and placed it under the rock shrine and whispered a prayer for the lost travelers.

Thinking that Nico might still be there at the site, he also left a small ham and cheese sandwich made with thinly sliced miga bread and a package of colorfully wrapped galletas, and a small bottle of water. Then he climbed up into the truck and pulled twice on the semi's thundering air horn to get Nico's attention as he drove away.

Nico watched the driver doing something for almost an hour as he worked at the roadside, then blasted his horn as he left. After a while, he wandered out and found the crude little religious shelter. He'd seen these most of his life, scattered along the roadways of Argentina where other people had been killed in car accidents, or where superstitious people left offerings to appease the saints that protected travelers, but he never really paid them much mind. Now he was looking down on what felt like his own crudely built little tombstone commemorating the place where he killed his family and where he was probably going to die himself very soon.

It was the first time since the car flew off the

mountainside that he felt any real emotion without the numbness that bound and gagged him. He felt a rage turning in his stomach, and threw his head back and his arms wide and screamed in the face of God. Four days worth of tears poured from his eyes and the veins in his temples bulged from beneath the skin as he yelled skyward. "Why did you do this!? I hate you, I hate you, I hate you!" He had to hate someone right now, and God is always where a man turns to expel his rage when he's alone in the world.

He realized now he had nothing left in his life but his great fortune, and it felt like an enormous burden. A gigantic, heavy bag of shit that he'd carried on his shoulders for much of his adult life. A weight that left him too weary at the end of the day to spend even a few minutes kicking a soccer ball around in his beautifully landscaped garden with his son, or make love to his lonely wife. And he had spent every single day of his life working feverishly to add to that bulging bag of shit. The wealth of the world could not offer him a moment's peace now, and the emotions he'd been holding down for the last four days were bursting.

As well as the anger and pain, he also suddenly felt the gut-wrenching hunger and thirst of sitting for days with no food or water, and he pounced on the offerings left in the little shrine by the truck driver. He shredded the paper wrappings and flung them to the wind and engulfed the sandwiches and cookies, then drank the bottle of water in a single gurgling breath. Then he looked around like a guilt stricken altar boy who just stole and drank the blood of Christ from the golden chalice on the church altar when no one was watching, and he fled back across the sandy hills to the safety of the wreckage and scurried through the open rear window.

He curled himself up on the back seat and sobbed and moaned. His cries echoed inside the crushed remains of the Mercedes, and all along the river's edge in the valley the animals and birds paused and looked to the east, and wondered what poor creature had just met its end. When his tears ran dry, the exhaustion of only a few hours of tortured sleep for days gripped him, and he fell fast asleep inside his rusting metal coffin.

Nico came awake in the last half hour of daylight, with a grinding pain. The small bit of food and water had made his stomach hurt, and he felt the acidy reflux come to the back of his throat and the urge to vomit into the floorboard, but he refused to let it come up. He felt the will to survive now. To live on and defy God's obvious desire for him to die.

He slid himself back out through the window and remembered the fish hanging over the cold fire, but almost nothing was left after the ants and birds had seen the free meal. A glint of reflected orange color from the last rays of the sun caught his attention. It was the shining coffee can and fishing line that Pablito had dropped to the sand and left without.

"If he could catch fish with this, so can I," he said to himself.

Nico looked around for something to bait the little hook with, but the only thing that caught his eye was a fat little black carpenter ant sifting through the greasy ashes of the fire. He grabbed it up and pinched it lightly until he heard the hard body crack, and then pierced it with the rusty little hook.

He could still see the remnants of worn and faded thread tied across the back of the hook, where it was once a beautiful imitation of a minnow or a flying insect. It probably belonged to some foreign fly fishing master, traveling along the banks of the Limay in search of legendary brown trout, and ended up tangled in the brushy thickets and given up for lost before being rescued by Pablito. Nico didn't really care where it came from, he just wanted a meal.

The sun was just falling behind the Andes range to the west, and the Lanin Volcano turned orange in the fading light and cast a fiery shadow on the river. He squinted into the reflections on the water and could see the circular ripples of trout gently sipping bugs from the surface in the middle of the river. He walked slowly to the edge and found a spot only 30 feet from the feeding fish and surveyed the water for his target.

He held the bottom of the coffee can with his left hand and pulled off some line with his right, and gave it a few swings around in a circle close to his body and sent it sailing out to the river, but the little hook and ant had almost no weight to them and after a few feet of line came off the can, the hook went slack in the air and flopped into the water in front of him. When he pulled it back in he was relieved to see that the little black ant, his only bait, was still clinging to the hook, so he pulled off a another three or four feet of line this time, and gave it big smooth arching swings and focused intently on the spot in the river.

This time, the little hook and ant flew farther into the river. Not quite where he wanted, but he decided to let it stay and float gently in the current for a few moments anyway. His father taught him to fish when he was a boy and he knew that fish can be many places in the river, and sometimes you just have to be confident.

He could see the fishing line floating along with the current as the hook and ant had disappeared and sank. Then he noticed the line paused, ever so slightly against the current. There wasn't a tug or pull on the line, only a barely imperceptible change in the way the line moved across the water.

He slowly pulled back on the line with his right hand until it tightened, and felt the frantic head shaking of a trout as the hook set into its jaw. He pulled it in hand over hand, and it jumped from the water into the air and flailed against the biting hook before Nico pulled it straight up onto the rocks and pounced on it with both hands. It was wet and slippery and squirming, so he whacked its head against a sharp stone, and it stiffened and curled its quivering tail forward in a final gasp before going limp.

It was the first trout he had caught in many years. A beautifully chromed rainbow with faint spots and rosy cheeks that stood out in the evening light, and it made him feel powerful for a moment, like he'd struck back against an angry world that was beating him down.

He used the matches that Pablito conveniently forgot, and built a small fire with twigs and dried grass. Then added the wood of a rotting acacia tree, uprooted and killed the year before by the muddy winter snow floods. Then he skewered the fish with a green willow branch through the gills and hung it over the flames. He squatted down low with his feet flat and his bottom resting on his heels, arms wrapped tightly around his knees for balance, like the pose the aboriginals take for endless hours when they're patiently waiting for some dangerous creature they wounded to draw up in the thick brush and bleed out.

He watched and listened to the flesh of this wonderful little piece of nature searing in the heat. Then devoured it, crunching through the fine wispy bones and leaving nothing but the spine and tail dangling from the charred head and blackened eyes. He put another few branches on the fire to build it up against the cold night air that he was feeling for the first time, and sat back against the rear wheel of the car and stared into the flames.

"I'm sorry I never taught you how to fish," he said,

as he saw Cristian's face in the flames. "I didn't even remember to bring a fishing rod to teach you with this year."

Cristian was so excited to go on this trip, and he knew this would be the year his father would wade him into the river and teach him to cast the elegant fly rods he kept neatly locked away in the closet at home. He loved other sports too, like football, but his grandfather used to tell him stories of fishing in the mountain streams in Italy and France. He also told him about teaching Nico to fish in the rivers north of Buenos Aires. He'd even been allowed to see and hold the bamboo fly rod that Gerard made years ago in Italy when he was a young man. He thought it looked like the beautiful wand of a magician.

"Do you think I'll have one like this someday, Papa?" he asked Nico.

"This one will be yours someday. But it's not for using in the river, it's too valuable." Nico said out loud to the crackling fire, as he recalled the conversation with his boy. "I'll get you something more simple to start with, then you can choose your own when you're older."

Nico felt the waves of guilt washing over him from unfulfilled promises. The burden of the living as they mourn the lost is being forever consumed by the things never said, the things never done, and all of the things that will never be.

He could hear his own father's voice in his head, and

could see him standing with him in the El Tigre river when they first came to Buenos Aires, and speaking so softly as he taught him to cast to the sea fish that came in with the ocean tide. He talked about casting a fly rod like a painter talks about creating art. But even as a boy, Nico was always a better fisherman than his father. He was born to it. His father's real talent was crafting the rods.

GERARD WAS JUST a boy growing up in a small village on the outskirts of Turin, in northwestern Italy near the French border when the first great war broke out and engulfed Europe. He was too young to fight and too old to sit at home while his family starved, so he did what he knew how to do; he went into the forests and mountains near his home and foraged, and he developed a particular talent for catching the trout that lived in the rivers and streams.

He learned to collect hooks and lures lost by other fishermen along the brushy banks of the Po river during the dry months when all of the underbrush and tangles were exposed above the water line. They were rusting and worn, but the fish didn't care.

He would find remnants of finely spun silk fishing line tangled among the trees and weave them together to make a length of six or seven meters, and secure it to the end of a stripped and dried willow branch. He would spin the bough deftly in his hands to wind the line around for safe keeping, and could just as quickly reverse the spin to free the line for a cast to a trout as he stalked along the shore.

Out of necessity, he learned the ways of the river and the creatures that lived there. Necessity teaches many young men the most valuable lessons of their lives.

One day, Gerard encountered a man along the stream who would change the course of his life, and the life of the son he didn't even know he would have someday. He was easing along the shore and made a cast to a trout rising behind a boulder in the stream, and the trout took his bait and was in his hand only seconds later, when he was startled by a clap and a cheer from the woods behind him.

He was frightened at first because he rarely saw anyone else in these woods, and these were dangerous times. It was another fisherman, an older man with a fancy looking rod and finely woven trout basket around his shoulders who saw him and cheered his success. Then he came down to the edge to congratulate him on a well played catch.

"Well done," the man said. "You're an expert fisherman."

"Thank you, sir," young Gerard responded warily. He looked the man over carefully as he approached and noticed the tailored outdoorsman clothes and his woven trout basket, and his beautiful fishing rod with a shining metal reel. He had the appearance of a gentleman, so he didn't feel threatened.

"I've been doing this for years with much more expensive equipment, but never seen it done any better. May I see that wonderful rod you're using?" the stranger asked.

Gerard held out his homemade willow branch rod, and the man laid his own fancy looking rod against a tree and accepted Gerard's carefully with both hands, as if he were holding something worth a great deal of money.

He slid his hand along the length and held it up to his eye and looked carefully down the edge, then whipped it back and forth a few times and commented on how well balanced it was, and how it flexed nicely in the hand.

"A very impressive piece of fishing equipment. Did you make it yourself?" he asked.

"Yes, sir."

The elderly fisherman it turned out, had once been considered the finest craftsman of rods made especially for the art of fishing with artificial flies. His rods had been purchased and used by the royals of Spain and Andorra, and he was famous among the avid fly fishermen of Belgium and Austria where his bamboo cane rods were highly coveted for their quality and beauty.

He moved to Turin at the beginning of the war to live with his family, and he was doing basically the same thing Gerard was doing up here in the mountains, bringing home a little extra food in the best way he knew how.

The old man hadn't worked much at building rods since the war started, but the war was nearing its end and he suspected he might have more business at hand soon, and thought maybe he could use an apprentice.

"Building fishing rods has been my business for many years young man, and I know a talented craftsman when I see one. I think I'll be back to building fly rods very soon as this war ends, and I could use a hand in my workshop. Would you consider coming to help me from time to time?" he said to Gerard.

Young Gerard glanced over at the gleaming elegant bamboo fly rod leaning against the tree and said, "Real fishing rods? I don't know anything about that, sir."

"That's what being an apprentice is all about. Your job would be to learn, and mine to teach. How about it?"

"It would be an honor, sir!" Gerard replied.

Gerard spent the next twelve years working for a few hours each afternoon, and learning in the old man's shop, and eventually he started developing a reputation as a master rod crafter himself. He loved the work more than anything he had ever done. After he finished secondary school he took a job working at a fine furniture shop in town, and he was good at that too and it paid very well, but his true love was making and casting these elegant fly fishing rods.

In the spring of 1939, a prince from the royal family in Belgium made contact with the legendary old rod builder and asked for something very special to be built for a fishing expedition to a mountainous land by the Black Sea that is now called Montenegro. A place with grand wild rivers and large hungry trout that demanded a rod much stronger and more powerful than most. The old man directed him to Gerard and said, "This is the young man you want to build it. He's a true master of the fly rod."

Gerard received a commission to build this custom fly fishing rod for the prince, using the finest bamboo cane from Asia, cork for the grip from the oaks of the southern French Alps, and engraved silver work from an Andalusian silversmith. It would be the rod that launched his career and brought him fame.

He spent months working late every night on the rod and completed the final finishing work on the 1st of September, 1939. The same day Germany invaded Poland. Britain and France entered the war two days later, and all hell broke loose across Europe. The Belgian prince was never heard from again. The masterpiece Gerard spent months working on stayed in a beautiful leather bound case on the top of his mantle for the next four and a half years until he found passage for himself, his wife and his young son, Nicholas, on a cargo ship coming to South America.

He accepted it as fate, that he should stick with the profession that earned him the most money, making fine furniture; and he would keep this rod, the one and only expression of his artistic soul, to pass down as his heirloom to his son when he was ready.

Gerard loved fishing until the day he died, and he taught the art of casting and understanding the way of the rivers to Nicholas and his friend Jorge when they were young, along the rivers and inland waterways near Buenos Aires. Nicholas was a natural, and he was passionate about fly fishing, but every year that he grew older he started to resent the hardships of living in poverty in the city a little more, and he focused his energy on understanding business and making money.

In time, the beautiful bamboo rod, made for a prince, became less of a symbol of his passion for fishing and pride in his father's accomplishment, and he thought of it as merely a valuable asset to be tucked safely away and guarded.

THINKING about his father gave Nico an idea. He remembered those stories about making a long casting rod from dried willow branches and abandoned line, and as he surveyed his surroundings he realized he had everything he needed.

The coffee can had worked fine, but he would never be as good with it as the gaucho, and he thought a rod would be easier for him to cast more precisely because he knew how to use a rod to swing and cast line. He could take the line and hook off the can and use that, and the river bank was lined with willow trees so he should be able to find a suitable branch for a rod.

He set out early the next morning in search of the perfect tree branch for his fishing rod. What he found was even better than willow. In this part of Patagonia, the cane plants, close relatives of the Asian bamboo, grow in huge bundles along the moist areas of streams and rivers where the shade covers them from the burning sun. Every twelve years, the cane plants flower, the one and only time in their lives, to spread their seeds to the wind and then die. The stalks turn brown and dry into a strong but flexible staff, up to fifteen feet long. It would make a perfect poor man's fishing rod.

Nico found a straight dried cane, and bent it over from the bottom and jumped up and down on top of it until it snapped off, then he ground the jagged broken bottom on a river stone until it was smooth. He stripped the small dried leaf shoots all along the length, then took the fishing line and the hook from the coffee can and tied it securely to the tip of the cane rod.

As he stood at the water's edge and practiced making sweeping round loops with the new cane pole rod and landed his hook nearly anywhere on the river he desired. He smiled and thought about his father. Gerard had helped feed his own family so many years ago in exactly the same way. He would have been proud that Nico remembered, and was using the memory to keep himself alive.

Survival

❧

From inside the smashed and cramped backseat, the early morning sounds of the desert were clear and sharp. The river's constant rushing and gurgling over and around the rocks, the wings of sparrows fluttering from bush to bush chasing morning mayflies, and the occasional splash of a trout chasing minnows into the shallow water.

The air was cool enough that Nico could see his own breath in a misty fog, but he was curled in a tight ball on the leather bench seat and once it warmed and softened up to his body heat it felt very fine, and he wasn't in any big hurry to leave the comfort of the warm spot. Unfortunately, nature was calling and he had to force himself out of the confines of the wreck to relieve himself.

He stood stiff-kneed in front of a sage bush squinting into the orange sunlight and watered it, then he raised his arms to stretch but his ribs sent a lightning bolt of pain through his body, and he hunched forward and groaned and took shallow breaths like he was breathing through a straw. The numbness of shock and adrenaline and pain relievers had worn off now, and his mind was starting to process everything he felt, both in his heart and in his slightly broken body.

He always faced east in the morning, in the direction of Buenos Aires, but he didn't feel any particular calling back to the city, he just enjoyed watching the sun rise. He used to do it in front of the waterway in Buenos Aires sometimes.

He would always rise early for work and leave the house to drive to his office at the factory, and on occasion, he would stop at the port and watch the sun come up over the ocean horizon and it made him feel like the world was coming alive with new possibilities. The black night sky would ease to gray, and then a faint orange glow rose in an arc before the sun sparkled at the border between the water and sky, and when the first full rays of sun landed on his face they were warm and fresh.

Now it just felt empty and cold. He wished he could stay curled in the warm spot on the leather back seat and sleep forever.

He turned around slowly and looked up the mountain side to the serpentine road above and noticed the gouges and scars in the gravel and rock face coming down, and places where the brush was torn out in a dotted path. Then he turned more to the west and saw a man cresting the hill and moving in his direction, and wondered for a second if it was the short gaucho, come back to run him off the land.

But this person was coming on foot, and a gaucho would never be coming here on foot. This man was stumbling through the thorns and thicket with a large bag slung across his shoulders, looking a little lost, and stopping and holding his hand up to block the sun in his eyes to recalculate his direction. Nico could tell by the way he moved that it was his friend Jorge.

He came slogging through the sand and bushes and dropped the large black canvas duffle bag onto the ground, completely winded from lugging the supplies across the terrain. Office work and city living had ruined him physically. He was panting and sweating, but he looked up at Nico with his usual smiling face, like it was any other day before. Then he glanced down and saw the cooling ashes from the fire and the charred evidence of the trout.

"I came back as fast as I could because I thought you'd be frozen or starving by now, but it looks like I didn't need to worry at all. And it looks like you had fresh trout for dinner last night. How did you manage that?"

"With a coffee can," Nico said, uttering his first complete sentence in four days.

"What? You'll have to teach me how to do that someday."

Jorge walked over to him and wrapped his arms around his best friend and squeezed him tight, and said, "I'm glad you're still alive, Nico."

Jorge wasn't filled with confidence when he left Nico a day and a half ago that he would still be alive when he came back, but he knew he couldn't have dragged him away from this place with an army, and the best he could do was leave him here to fend for himself and get back as quick as he could with some supplies to stay a while. Maybe he'd be ready to leave now, maybe in a few days more, but Nico needed to be ready to leave in his own time.

By the time Jorge reached San Martin de Los Andes, it was late in the evening and everything was closed, so he had to stay the night. He needed a good night's rest anyway, and while he spent much of it worrying about Nico huddling in the back of the wreckage, he still managed a little sleep.

The next day he bought clothes, a tent and sleeping bags, a small gas stove and a cooking tin and coffee pot, and some basic camping tools. Then he bought groceries, mostly canned foods and sausages, and several bottles of Quilmes beer.

He filled his car with gas at the YPF station on the way out of town, and when he went inside to pay he noticed it. In the corner next to the beer cooler, was a wooden stand with a lonely fiberglass fly fishing rod standing upright. It was a cheap model meant for a passing tourist, and had probably been there for years waiting for someone to take it home, but it was a ready kit with a reel and two spools of line and a little box of artificial flies hanging from a tether.

Without really knowing why, he bought the rod and took it apart and tucked it neatly into the big bag of supplies.

"I thought we might be camping out here for a while so I bought a few things," he said. "I'll set up camp."

Nico wandered down to the river while Jorge opened the duffle bag and started setting out the tent and poles and gear, and he pulled the fly rod out and connected the pieces back together and leaned it against the Mercedes where Nico would see it. Nico saw the rod when he came back later that evening but he didn't touch it, and said nothing about it, and didn't mention to Jorge that he had fashioned his own cane rod.

The two friends spoke only a handful of words to each other for the rest of the day and that night because it really wasn't necessary, it was a time to be quiet and think. Nico thinking about Marie and Cristian, and Jorge thinking about how to manage the businesses back in the world and take care of his friend here until he was ready to leave, although he still harbored a little hope that Nico would come around and be willing to drive back home with him in a few days.

That first night, Jorge had the tent pitched and fire blazing. He gathered a large cache of dried wood that was neatly deposited all along the high water mark of the river and piled it close to camp while Nico wandered along the river's edge in solitude.

He knew Nico would find his way back with the fire lighting a beacon in the darkness, and he kept a can of food warm over the side of the coals in the tin pot, and had river-chilled beer waiting when Nico came into camp an hour after sunset. Jorge had anchored the beer in a deep swirling pool behind a boulder in the river where the cold mountain water would keep it chilled. He'd also picked up some cheap rubber boots in town to keep from ruining his dress shoes any more than they already were, and they kept his feet dry while he was retrieving beer from nature's cooler.

"I kept dinner warm for you, but you might enjoy the beer more," Jorge said as he walked up.

"Thanks. You're a good friend. You've always been a good friend," Nico said.

The camp fire dwindled and the waxing moon rose and cast shadows on the mountainous terrain and turned the river into a shimmering road in the darkness that wandered to the east. The night sounds and rushing water all became amplified as if their sense of hearing was sharper when eyesight failed in the darkness, and the smoke from the fire dulled their sense of smell.

The two friends had spent many nights just like this camped near the El Tigre when they were boys. Sparring and joking around the fire until the night reached its zenith of darkness and the fire faded, then everyone around it falls into their own personal silent reflection. As boys grow to men, it's the final moment when they take stock of the day, and revel in their victories or absorb the pain of defeat.

Jorge ended the silence, "I'm off to sleep, my friend. The tent is big enough for both of us, but you can bring your sleeping bag outside if you want to be under the stars tonight."

"I want to be out here tonight, but I'll take the bag," Nico said.

He was still wanting to be in the backseat of the Mercedes at night. As cramped as it was, it made him feel close to Cristian and he wasn't ready to leave that feeling behind yet. Jorge pulled the bag out for him, then zipped himself into the tent, and was sound asleep in minutes.

Nico sat outside alone for some time, and for a few moments his mind went peacefully blank, completely engrossed in the moonlight and the whispers of desert animals. He knew in that moment that the only peace he was going to find from all of this would be found here, or nowhere.

When sleepiness finally came to him, he pushed the bag through the open window first, then crawled into the back seat and wrapped himself in the goose down bag and slept soundly. He dreamed of his father and the nights he and Jorge spent so many years before under the open sky.

The next two days passed much the same. They

would wake and start a small fire to boil some water and make coffee. Then Nico spent his days wandering down to the river's edge to be alone, and sometimes taking his cane pole with him to fish. He would gather a few of the freshly hatched insects that landed on the rocks and shrubs at the river's edge and put them in his shirt pocket, and thread them gently onto the fine rusty hook when he felt like making a cast.

As much as Jorge wanted to care for his friend, he started realizing that he couldn't do it here, and Nico would not be leaving anytime soon. He had to make other arrangements now, both for Nico and for the businesses that were left unattended. On the third day he made his decision to go back to Buenos Aires.

He was starting the fire again in the late afternoon to make mate when Nico came back into camp. "I'll be leaving in the morning for Buenos Aires, Nico," He said, still clinging to the smallest hope that Nico might want to come back with him.

"Yes, you should be back there. Your life is there, Jorge," Nico replied.

Jorge looked out over the river and he could see the afternoon hatch starting of the huge yellow mayflies that come up in the willow trees this time of year in Patagonia. They looked like a wispy golden smoke that hovered over the river, and he could see the trout rolling restlessly on the surface and anticipating the little morsels falling into the water.

"I'd love to fish this river with you some day, Nico.

You could teach me how to cast to those rising browns in the fast water." Jorge was talking to himself more than Nico, and he was secretly worried that Nico may have died in that crash too; he just didn't know he was dead yet. He knew the best he could do for his friend right now was to find some way to help him from a distance, and make sure everything he'd worked for his whole life was still there when he wanted to come back. If he ever wanted to come back.

He knew Nico better than anyone alive, including what Nico needed in his life at any given moment. And he could tell clearly what Nico needed right now. He needed to be alone, with nothing to remind him of the outside world or his obligations. His only obligation now was to be here in this place, and whether he survived or died would have to be his choice.

You can't force a man to keep living, if he can't find something on his own that he cares enough about to live for. It's a harsh truth, but the most loving thing you can do for a man sometimes is allow him to suffer and fight to pull himself out of the darkness.

"Nico, don't think about anything else except what you have to do here. I'll take care of everything back in Buenos Aires. I need to go now, but I'll be back here very soon to check on you, and I'll bring more supplies when I can."

Nico stayed rolled in the sleeping bag in the back of the Mercedes later the next morning. He could hear Jorge getting up and making a coffee before he gathered his bag of dirty clothes and walked off through the brush towards the highway where he left his car. There wasn't anything for them to say to each other that hadn't already been said, or that they already knew in their hearts.

THE CHEAP FIBERGLASS fly rod that Jorge bought and left standing upright against the Mercedes had been blown over by the wind during the night, and was now laying half buried in the sand. Nico had ignored it for three weeks, not because he didn't appreciate the gift from his friend, but because it reminded him of something he didn't want to deal with right now. It felt like something he'd given up years ago when it was time to give up childish ways and become a man, and it also reminded him of promises he made to his son that he never made good on. But today was different.

When he noticed the cheap little rod laying on the ground, which is a horrible thing for any fisherman to see, he felt pity for it, like it was an abandoned creature left to fall to the earth and die a lonely death.

He could hear his father's voice in his head, "Don't ever leave a rod lying on the ground where it can be stepped on and broken!"

Nico walked over and reached down and pulled the rod from the sand and the bright yellow finish glistened in the morning sun. He gripped it by the handle and gave it a shake to loosen the grit and sand from the reel, and the energy from his hand pulsed through the length of the shaft and he could feel it breathing life into the rod as it waved back a forth, then dissipated back to stillness.

It had been so long since he held a fly rod in his hands that he'd forgotten. He'd forgotten how something inanimate can come to life in the hands of someone who understands it, and even though he hadn't been on the river in a long time, this was a gift that Nico was blessed with from the beginning.

"Teach me to fish today, Papa," he heard the voice say. He looked up, and there was Cristian standing in front of him. A faint shimmering specter, but clearly there. "Please. Take me to the river," he said. Then the apparition smiled and faded away as it turned to the Limay.

"Today is the day, Cristian," he said to the vanishing boy. Then he set to work, preparing the rod for his son.

Nico took the knife that Jorge left for him and clipped the string that bound the little fly reel, then pulled out several meters of the heavy fishing line and carefully threaded it through the wire guides along the length of the rod and out the tip. Then he opened the little tethered box to see what assortment of artificial flies were tucked inside.

It contained a total of ten, composed of two tiny mayfly imitations, three that resembled silvery little minnows with light green feathers over their back, and five that looked like some dark ugly water bug that he wasn't familiar with. None of them appeared very professionally prepared, but they had sharp hooks and he thought if the fish weren't fooled by them, then he could just cut off the feathers and material and bait the hooks with real ants or grasshoppers or something.

He walked up the hill to a large rock that had a commanding view of the river, and he sat on top of it for a long time just watching the water flow and reading the river. After a while he started seeing the river the way an experienced fisherman sees it; in channels and foam lines, and seams where two currents meet, in eddies and pools and deep water drop-offs, and shade and structure where the big fish lay waiting for prey.

He could see that the flying insect hatch that happens in the early morning hours had passed, so the bigger fish were feeding deeper and he could see a line of foam and debris floating close to the edge where medium sized fish were plucking dead bugs as their bodies gathered in little floating rafts.

"That's where we'll get our fish today, Cristian. Right there in that foam line. We'll try one of these ugly bugs first," he said.

He tied an ugly bug to the thin tippet at the end of his line, then slowly approached the river and calculated the distance to the foam line and pulled some line out from the reel to start the cast. Nico could feel Cristian's thin body pressing against him, his small hand gripping the cork handle beneath his. "We'll do it together," he whispered into his son's ear.

He slowly pulled the rod up and back over his right shoulder and pressed it forward in a smooth motion. Then he drew it backward again and pulled more line free from the reel, and focusing intently on the place in the water he wanted to land the fly, he pressed it firmly forward again and the line soared past him in an elegant loop and unfolded in the air and lit softly on the water. "Wasn't that easy?" he said, as he saw Cristian turn his head and smile.

He let the little ugly bug float freely along in the foam, surrounded by the carcasses of hundreds of other bugs that ended their lives in the river, until it passed downstream of him; then he gently raised the rod tip high in the air and with one circular wave of the wand he landed it back to its original starting point.

This time, as the ugly bug floated over a stretch of rocks that looked particularly fishy, he reached up with his left hand and tapped the lower section of the rod as a musician might tap the strings of a guitar along the fretboard, and the resulting shock in the rod sent a quiver all the way down through the line, and made the bug at the end wiggle so slightly that it made only the tiniest imperceptible ripple on the surface.

In an instant, a trout bolted from the rocky bottom and seized the ugly bug fly in its mouth, and with a splash of its tail, turned and rushed straight back down to the deep water. Nico pulled the line tight with his left hand and gently raised the rod tip until he felt the shiny little hook set hard into the fish's mouth, and he watched the rod bounce and dance under the weight of the trout as it rushed back and forth in the current. When the fish tired, he gently pulled it close enough to kneel down in the water and grasp it around its belly and lift it up into the light.

Yes, he really had forgotten. Not just how alive an inanimate fly rod could feel in his hands; but how alive it made him feel as well. The rod was like a conduit that connected him to the river and awakened the most natural part of his being. Standing knee-deep in the rushing water with the current pressing against his legs and conducting an orchestral rhythm with the creatures that dwelled below, he transformed just as Pablito had when he mounted his speckled grey horse.

He became 'something else'. His own version of an elemental.

He took a moment to admire the beautiful little fish, with its metallic bronze body and crimson red spots encircled by blue and yellow rings. It was a brilliantly painted piece of nature. Were it not for the fact that he was desperately hungry he would have released it back to the river to keep growing, but this was purely predatory now, with no more malicious intent than the trout itself had when it lunged to consume the hapless ugly bug floating on the surface.

"I'm sorry I have to kill you, my little friend. But this is what I do," he said.

He expelled its life-force quickly, and lay the trout up on the bank under a shady bush. Then he continued the quest for another to put enough food in his stomach to survive the day. As he stood in the edge of the water he heard the clacking and splashing of hooves coming along the rocky waterline.

The gaucho, Pablito, had returned to see if the Porteño, as city people from Buenos Aires are often called in the provinces, was still squatting on his section of the estancia.

He left his puesto early again this morning and traveled a well worn trail down to the river, turned east and followed the shore for a mile until he reached a wide shallow *vado*, and urged his horse across the swift current to the other side. Then he followed the high water line for another three miles, parallel to the roadway but far enough to remain hidden from the noisy automobiles and trucks and double deck buses, until he came to the place where the Mercedes had fallen.

The sight of Nico catching his breakfast wasn't exactly what he hoped to find. Now he was faced with a decision that he always hated to make. Be polite, or be fierce.

* * *

PABLO GONZALEZ HAD LIVED and worked his entire life within the bounds of the private estancia that bordered the Limay river and spread out west and north farther than his eyes could see. His father and mother had also lived and worked most of their lives for the French owners of this incredible land mass, tending a puesto, a small outpost, hidden in a spring-fed meadow between two hills that blocked the never ending wind. This had been the original homestead site of the pioneering family from France more than 100 years before, and the trees they planted then now stood like towers around the small wooden cabin.

Pablito was born in that cabin, and grew up playing in the fields and hills, learning to tend to horses and cattle under the watchful eye of his father, and also learning the ways of the land and the river that flowed through the estancia. He marveled at the huge trout that swam in the river and knew their feeding and migrating habits as well as he knew the patterns of wind and weather that dictated their lives in the open spaces of Patagonia.

He spent most days dressed in basically the same clothing, because he owned so few things, and really needed nothing more than what he owned. He wore thick bombacha pants, pleated at the waist and forgiving in the seat, with legs that opened and buttoned at the bottom to make them easy to get into and wear either over or under the length of his boots. They were sturdy and hard against the thorny brush; made for men who spent most of their lives perched in a saddle and meandering across the open pampas.

On warm sunny days he wore a long sleeved cotton shirt that was usually blue, and on cold or rainy days he draped an elegant poncho over himself that his wife made for him the first year they were married. He always wore a brown scarf with a small stag antler clasp around his neck, and a boina hat to protect his head from the wind and sun.

Like the rugged landscape around him, Pablito had been shaped and carved by the elements over time. His skin was thick and creviced from the wind and seasonal heat or cold, and many hours a day spent atop a sheep skin lined saddle left him with a stiff gate on foot.

His hands always looked horribly swollen and battered, with fingers twice the diameter of a normal man, even though he stood barely five feet and four inches. Working with livestock and wire and all manner of tools every day strengthens and distorts the bones and muscles in the hands.

Despite his rough appearance, he had a deep kindness about him. He sensed the needs of people and animals alike, and he cared without even knowing why. He was just born with a natural empathy for living things. It was this empathy that drew him instantly to Nico.

* * *

PABLITO WAS ALWAYS TOLD by his administrator to forcefully drive away anyone that trespassed within the bounds of the estancia, and a number of poachers had learned this diminutive gaucho was not one to be trifled with. But as he reckoned it, Nico and his wrecked car and his camp were all technically below the seasonal high water mark of the river at the present time, and by law, everyone has free access to the river below that mark. It seemed a reasonable assessment to be polite, rather than forceful.

"Buen día, Señor," he said as he approached on his horse.

"Buen dia." Nico responded.

They stared at each other in an awkward silence for a long time, Nico looking up, and Pablito looking down from a dominant posture aboard his gray horse, which eventually broke the gaze by shuffling his hooves and twisting sideways to a position on the rocks that was less bothersome for his legs. As the eye contact was interrupted, Nico said, "I was about to make some mate." It was a polite social invitation that couldn't be refused.

Nico tended to building a fire and starting to boil water in a tin pot that Jorge had bought, while Pablito led his horse to a deadfall tree and tied his reigns. He was taking careful notice of everything that had changed since he first came to check the site weeks earlier. He noticed there was now a tent, and equipment used for camping and cooking, and of course, he noticed the new fly fishing rod in Nico's hands when he approached him at the river. He was concerned, but cautious about confronting him.

As soon as the fire was safely burning without being tended, Nico walked to the canvas bag by the tent and pulled out the coffee can fishing apparatus, and respectfully handed it back to Pablito.

"You forgot this when you were here before. I hope you don't mind, but I used it once or twice to catch a fish for dinner," he said. "I also put on new line and a hook for you."

They both knew that the coffee can being left was not an accident, but it made Nico feel better to return it, and Pablito felt good that his gesture had been noticed and appreciated. He smiled, and accepted the can, and walked back to his horse and tucked it safely into the wool bag, after removing a small bundle. He came back to the fire pit and pulled up a tree trunk and sat on it, then opened the bundle and revealed half a dozen fresh biscuits that his wife made in the wee hours of the morning, and stuffed into his bag for the ride out.

He leaned across the fire and mate pot and offered Nico the first, and he reached in and took one. The biscuit was round and lumpy with a golden crust on top, and he gently broke the crust open, pulled it apart, and brought it up close to his nose. The wonderful fresh doughy aroma reminded him of his mother. He could see her in his mind, working in the kitchen every morning before anyone else in the house was awake yet, cooking scones or fresh bread for Gerard to take with him to the shop.

Nico took a small bite and pressed it lightly against the roof of his mouth with his tongue and gently rolled it as it softened and melted before he swallowed. It was the most common of foods in the campo, and still, it gave him a moment of serenity in reflection. He smiled ever so faintly, and lightly nodded his head to let Pablito know that it was an enjoyable pleasure.

When the water was hot, Nico prepared mate in Jorge's fancy gourd and handed it to Pablito. He knew that his visit was about more than biscuits and mate, so he spoke while Pablito silently sipped from the bombilla.

"A friend came looking for me, and he brought these things from San Martin de Los Andes to stay with me for a few days. He's gone back to Buenos Aires now," Nico said.

Pablito glanced around at the tent and gear bag, but said nothing. Nico looked into his eyes and realized there was more that needed to be said.

"My wife and my son are here. I can't leave them." Was all he could think of to say. His eyes spoke volumes more than the few words. They begged for understanding from the gaucho. They begged to find some understanding in everything that was happening to him.

Pablito looked intently at Nico, then nodded his head to show that he understood both what he was saying, and what he was feeling. He didn't know what he was going to tell the owner of the estancia when he was asked about the man at the river, but he had no intentions of driving him away at the point of a blade. He thought maybe the owner would eventually call the provincial Gendarmerie to come take him, but as long as he stayed below the high water mark he was safe for now.

As he stepped up to his horse and prepared to leave, he thanked Nico for the mate, and Nico thanked him for the fresh biscuits and gave his best compliments to his wife's cooking. It would be the first of many breakfasts and mate the two would share together in the coming months.

The Demon

❧

The full weight of summer bore down on the mesa and the leading edge of the river valley below, where the Mercedes lay rusting and cooking on the rocks. Searching for Buenos Aires on the eastern horizon in the early morning hours yielded a rippling heat mirage, distorting the rising sun into a waving flame.

There was little shade on the river bank, save for the scattered willows on the opposite shoreline, and up river where the rows of poplars were planted for wind deflection generations ago. The mountains grew in earnest only a few miles to the west where the rivers were born, and they beckoned with evergreens and summer fruit trees, and icy caps that stayed white until just before the autumn foliage began to turn. But where Nico remained with Marie and Cristian, it was hot. A flesh-searing, desiccating heat that would bring nothing but weakness, nausea, and death to any who lingered in it ill-prepared.

The next river system to the north was known by the aboriginals as the Cóllon Curá [hot rocks], because in the dead of summer the rocky shore would scald the feet of men and animals who came to drink. As the cool mountain water splashed up the bank and onto the black volcanic boulders they steamed and smoldered.

Nico spent the morning curled up in the sleeping bag and ignored the sunrise and the sweltering inferno that was building inside the tent. He'd had fitful dreams again the previous night about the faceless boy and the black-eyed demon lurking in the river below the willows in the deep channel on the far side.

The heat finally drove him out, and he used the little gas camp stove to brew some coffee, then sat staring up at the roadway as a couple of buses crawled down the road and continued farther south. They were delivering teenaged backpackers from the northern provinces and Buenos Aires, and a few foreign tourists coming to explore the great frontier at the end of the world. He decided this would be a good day to fish late, after the temperature fell and as soon as he started seeing the early evening's newly hatched mayflies fluttering in the poplars and willows along the shoreline.

Instead, he would spend the day walking. He would venture farther over the next hill to see the snow-covered tips of the Andes mountains jutting up from the western horizon, and see what the river might hold in the way of fishable pools farther upstream. He could check the little shrine on the way back for any charitable bits of food.

He walked four miles upriver to a place where the Limay was joined by a nameless stream that flowed down from a towering peak. Marie had seen eagles perched high up on its face many times as they passed this way.

She always begged him to stop the car and take photographs, but there was never time. There was never time for so many of the gentler influences of life. The smallest of gestures that slip through the fingers like grains of sand and are lost forever. It's the great lie that haunts us later when those grains turn to regrets. The lie that blames time when there is always time; but it's conscious choice that allows the grains to fall from our grasp.

The nameless stream was lined with poplars, and he napped in a bed of long, green grass in the cool shade and stared up at the mountain peak for most of the day before starting his hike back. The little shrine held a fortune. Two wrapped sandwiches and a tiny, single serving bottle of Malbec with a screw off top. He gobbled one of the sandwiches on the way back to his tent, and saved the other for later, in case he had no luck with the trout. He would savor the wine at night by the fire.

At seven in the evening, a light breeze started to blow and the freshly hatched insects were cast into the air from their sanctuaries amid the leaves and trees along the river. He could see the fish dabbling and kissing the surface of the water. He used one of the tiny mayfly imitations that came in the kit, and caught a fat little rainbow trout on the third cast.

When the sun starting sinking below the mountain over the Caleufu river to the west, he paused and watched it until it disappeared and left the puffy clouds overhead in an orange glow with a purple backdrop. He bent over and cupped his hands and filled them in the cold pure river and drank twice, and while he stood there looking at the mountain, it occurred to him that the three-hundred-thousand acres of timberland he owned were just on the other side.

"Look Marie, the sun is shining right this moment on our beautiful Oregon Pine trees," he said to her.

He could see her smiling face turn towards him in the fading sunlight, and her hair waving lightly in the afternoon breeze. That was always his favorite time of day here in Patagonia when they came every summer. He would have finished his work by now and come back to the house in the late afternoon, just in time to sit outside on the lawn and share a glass of Malbec with Marie, and see the fading light bring a flush of color to her flawless olive skin.

"One more little fish, and we'll have enough for dinner," he said to her.

He decided this time to move upstream a bit and give a rest to the foam line that he fished most of the time, and he entered the water in almost the same place where Pablito had caught two trout. He waded in to his knees and paused to read the water. He could see the telltale rings of sipping fish lips in a nice feeding chain on the far side, five or six trout lined up in a row below the overhanging willow trees. It was much farther than he could have reached with the coffee can or with his cane pole, but with the fiberglass rod he thought he could make the cast that far, so he pulled out line and made his cast and landed the fly where the current would soon carry it to the feeding fish.

It didn't take long. As the fly drifted under the first dark patch of shade, a small trout gently slurped it from the surface. He wasn't a particularly big fish, so Nico started pulling him in with the line in his left hand to get the fish in quickly, and the little trout came instinctively to the surface and thrashed to spit out the biting hook. What happened next would haunt Nico for a long time to come.

As the little fish flipped and thrashed on the surface, he drew the attention of something else in the deep water farther down the channel. Downstream of the fish, and all along the cut-bank below the overhanging willows the surface of the water boiled with frantic small fish trying to flee the area. Some even flew out of the water so fast they leapt upward into the overhanging tree limbs and became entangled for a few seconds before falling back with a splash.

Nico's eyes darted left at the commotion and he saw

a large black shadow racing forward against the current and pushing a bulging wave in front of it. It covered 30 feet in what seemed like less than a second, then drove straight down for an instant before turning back upward and attacking from below like an ocean predator, but this was a crystal green Andean river, not the ocean. It slammed into the little trout and seized it sideways in its gaping hooked jaw and flew clear of the water like a breaching shark and landed with a crash that sent water spraying nearly back to Nico across the river. It was easily three times the length of the trout in its mouth and its body had the girth of a man's thigh. It was dark and mottled, with fins that didn't look like fins anymore, but more resembled thick paddles with jagged ends. And the eyes; the eyes were what Nico had seen over and over in his nightmares as bottomless blackness with gold slits like a cat.

The river demon turned to the deep water and sank, its prize dangling limp in its teeth, but the tiny mayfly hook was still clinging to the little trout, and when the line came tight the demon jerked his head left and right, then powered deep with his oar-sized tail. Nico's fly rod bent nearly double and made a crackling noise like it was reaching its breaking point, when at once the line at the end snapped with the ring of a broken instrument string and came flying back at his face. Nico ducked as the line came whistling past, and stood for a second in a state of confusion. Was it real? Or was he having another nightmare?

Nico scrambled back to the safety of the shore and turned to look back to the far side of the river, but it was completely calm like nothing had ever happened.

"I've been seeing you in my dreams, and now you've come to taunt me in this world!" Nico yelled.

Then, in his head or from the water he couldn't tell, he heard the demon call back to him.

"Taunt? I have no need for taunts. I am the god of this flowing world. I hunt, I kill, and I devour all who dare enter my realm. The young, the old, the weak and strong; they all fall to my snapping jaws. This is what I do," the demon voice whispered. "I know you all too well, beast that crawls on the land. I see into the deep of you, and you are a killer too." Then, he laughed and faded into the darkest recess of the swirling pool below the willows.

It wasn't just a nightmare after all; the thing he was seeing as he slept was lurking here in the river with him. He was an adversary. He was challenging Nico's will to survive. And he wouldn't be the only one.

Jacques

Jacques d'Auvergne sat in a large black leather club chair pulled tightly into the corner of his private study, near the stone-lined fireplace with a huge hearth carved from richly grained roble wood. On top of the hearth were layers of photographs of his children and grandchildren, all neatly framed and arranged with specific partiality. There was an empty place in the center front of the arrangement, and the frame had been removed from its place long enough that the dust had covered any trace of its previous location. That photograph was resting in his lap.

He no longer sat tall and straight, as he demanded of his daughters and his fine grandson over the years. The terrible weight of mourning and depression had slowly compressed him into a gelatinous lump in the chair, with his shoulders drooped and his head hanging limply forward that his chin now rested on his sternum, and his feet had slid forward on the oak floors and lay extended and splayed outward.

The room was enormous and mostly open space with the exception of a scrolled mahogany desk topped in green leather, and the two matching club chairs on either side of the fireplace. The walls were dark wood paneled and covered with family portraits from four generations of the d'Auvergne lineage. Scalloped ceiling tiles and a small crystal chandelier added to the sense of grandeur, as did tall glass doors that opened into his private garden, but the thick golden shades had remained closed for a long time now, and the only light in the room was emanating from the flickering fire.

Jacques' face had lost its earthy olive complexion and was now the color of white-burned ash from weeks of seclusion in the darkened room. He had folded himself into this same chair for most of the days that had past since he buried his oldest and most promising daughter and his grandson in his family mausoleum in the famous Recoleta Cemetery.

It was a well represented funeral. His friends from the city counsel, the mayor of Buenos Aires, even the provincial governor had all attended. His other daughters returned from their lives abroad to say farewell to their sister. Porsche, who attended university in London and had married a successful English businessman; and Monique, who lived in Paris, but they left soon after. It was much the same group that had attended when he buried his wife little more than a year before. However, at this funeral there were people he didn't recognize, all from different parts of the city or other cities entirely. Friends and business associates of Nicholas.

In his mind, Marie represented his greatest legacy to the world. She was known and admired throughout the province and people frequently asked him about his lovely daughters, Marie in particular. She was the near image of her mother, whom Jacques had loved from the moment he met her, over thirty five years before.

Cristian was a bright and handsome grandson with scholarly promise, and he bore the d'Auvergne name as his secondary surname, but now it would likely fade from the records of history in Argentina, as Jacques never had a son of his own. His lack of a son had drawn him even closer to Nico over the past years, because Nico had treasured their time together, and held Jacques in the highest esteem.

Nico looked at Jacques as the father he sometimes wished he had been born to, rather than the poor immigrant father he had. He loved Gerard and was grateful for the things he learned from him as a boy, but his resentment for being poor as a child was a burden that Jacques could release him from, and when Gerard passed away, Nico gravitated completely to his father-in-law for guidance.

Jacques understood the benefits of wealth and influence, and since Nico had married his favorite daughter, he was willing to share the secrets with Nico to ensure their future, and his legacy.

Until he met Marie, Nico had been finding clients for his father's shop mostly one at a time by spending endless hours riding the bus into the city and walking from office to office with photographs. He found businessmen, bankers, and lawyers who were willing to order a custom chair or desk on occasion. The order to produce twelve custom park benches for the Botanical Gardens had come through a recommendation of a well connected banker. That banker also turned out to be an associate of Jacques.

Jacques had been the sole heir to a great deal of wealth. The d'Auvergne family had been an engrained part of Argentine society for generations and each successive generation had increased the family's worth. His financial and political connections afforded him the ability to grow that wealth without having to actually run a business or be engaged in regular work, but rather by keeping his assets strategically placed under the counsel of his friends and associates.

When Marie became formally engaged to Nico, despite his disapproval, he determined he could improve Nico's position in the community by bringing a grander scale to his business. He had engineers brought in to devise a plan to mass produce furniture in what would become Azzarà Industries, and bankers to finance the operation.

While it's true that Nico eventually led the

company to success and cleverly reinvested the profits into other assets, he had significant support from Jacques. The d'Auvergne name, and having Marie by his side also brought an instant level of legitimacy and acceptance to his success. He might have eventually made his own fortune without Jacques' assistance, but it would have still been regarded as "new" money, and while new money had purchasing power, it lacked influence. With a d'Auvergne heir by his side he now had the connections of old money. The kind of connections that lead you to fishing trips with the President.

Jacques' legacy and the influence of his name had been stolen from him by the man he treated as he would have a son.

Jorge came to the d'Auvergne residence nearly every week after the funeral, hoping to spend time with Jacques and deal with this tragedy together. This did not occur. Jacques refused any and all admittance to his study save the maid who provided food and brandy. Even she was permitted only in and out. She was not allowed to tidy the room, and over the days and weeks it took on the seedy air of thwarted love, though she spoke of this to no one.

Jorge had loved Marie as a sister and Cristian as much as if he were his own son, and he felt the same broken pieces falling loose inside him as Jacques and Nico. He was a more gregarious soul, and he desperately needed to be with someone to get through this, but the other two were different sorts of men. They were isolated and consumed by the grief, and wanted nothing but solitude.

There were also other matters that Jorge and Jacques would have to confront. Matters that would not continue to lay dormant much longer.

Jacques pulled himself forward in the leather chair and drew his feet under him and stood for the first time in several hours, and his feet were stinging and prickling from the sudden flow of oxygenated blood. He shuffled slowly to the doorway that lead out to the garden, still holding the photograph of Marie and Cristian in his hand, and pushed the curtain to the side just far enough to put his face to the opening.

The sunlight was blinding for a moment, and he squinted and blinked until his pupils contracted to bring the garden into focus. The first thing he saw clearly was the garden bench that Nico had given to Marie all those years ago, resting beneath a cascading wall of orange trumpet vine. It welled something deep inside him. His suffering had festered long enough to evolve into the next logical form, anger. No, not really anger. After laying eyes on the garden bench, it was more akin to a well fermented rage.

He felt the sudden shiver of adrenaline rushing through his veins, and his teeth began grinding back and forth as he stared at that goddamn bench. His hand holding the curtain was gripping tighter and tighter, until the curtain broke away from the rod and came crashing to the floor. Now the light of day poured into the study, and woke Jacques to a new mission in his life.

He was going to bring the full weight of his wrath down on Nico. Wherever he was, no matter what his condition, he was going to bring him to an end.

Enemies

The barrier between sanity and something less than sane, is a permeable membrane. The effects of shock, injury, grief, and barely enough food and sleep to sustain life were starting to push Nico into a place that wasn't always connected with the real world.

More than a month had passed since the accident, but he had no sense of time in this place. He lived in a perpetual state that contained only fragments of the past, with no concept of a future. Jorge had come again not many days past to bring more supplies, but Nico was tiring of his endless badgering to leave this place.

"Nico, you can't stay here forever. You need to come back to your life. There are businesses and people who depend on you!" He said.

"You care about it so much, ...take it," was Nico's response. He went on. "You should leave now Jorge, we don't want you here anymore."

It was the *we* that bothered Jorge the most. He'd seen Nico pissed off a lot of times in his life, and they'd had their fair share of disagreements, but this was something different. He was being pushed away by the counsel of phantoms.

Nico's mind was clinging so tightly to the ghost of Marie that it was pulling him into the realm where she now existed. Someplace other than the physical world. When he slipped into that place, he could see her face more clearly, hear her voice as if she were only inches away from him, and if he concentrated very hard he could almost feel the faint touch of her hands like a silky veil passing softly over his skin. He craved it more with every day that passed, like a drug highjacking his brain.

There were times he was drawn back to the physical present - when he was wading in the water and fishing for his dinner or engaging in basic chores of survival like gathering firewood, and when he had visitors who demanded his attention, which was only Jorge and the gaucho, Pablito. When he wandered the hills or shoreline of the river, and when he was alone at night by the fire or in his tent, he was with Marie.

It was during one of his daily wanderings that she whispered something dangerous in his ear.

"I'm here because of them," she said.

"Because of who?"

"Them. The ones up there."

He could see her icy blue eyes glaring up to the

twisting highway above them, and the endless train of trucks grinding up and down the road in slow motion.

"The trucks. I forgot about the trucks," he said.

"The truck killed me, Nico," he heard her say.

"What should I do, Marie?"

"You know what to do. You always know what to do." She whispered softly into his ear.

It was a moment of beautiful perfect insanity. A contorted version of reality that freed Nico from the overwhelming guilt. It wasn't his fault anymore. He didn't do it; they did.

He crawled to a higher vantage point and watched them for hours; engine-breaking their monstrous vehicles down the serpentine track on one side, and others roaring the engines at full power to climb on the other. There were rusty old cabs with flatbeds carrying pallets of bricks, and shiny new Macks with glistening stainless trailers, box vans and refrigerated food trucks, and the ones Nico now looked at as pure evil, the long flat haulers loaded with timber and lumber. He'd forgotten or didn't care anymore that some of that lumber being hauled up and down the road belonged to him.

He moved closer and closer to the roadway, looking for a pattern, a weakness, or an opportunity to strike out at his new enemy. Some of the heaviest trucks would reach the flat bottom and pull over for a few minutes to cool their brakes on the gravel shoulder, just across the road from his little shrine, so he stalked through the thorns up to the edge of the road. He watched and waited patiently, as he did each night before gliding into the river to make the first cast.

Two small box vans came into the pullout first, and they stopped and the drivers chatted, and smoked and shared a mate before leaving. They weren't the ones he was after. Then an old beat up truck loaded with fresh apples from the farmland in Cinco Saltas came to the stop, but the driver was an old feeble man with ragged clothes, and a noticeable limp, and Nico couldn't find any hatred in his heart for him.

Then from the last corner up the road, he heard it coming; engine rapping down the hill and the brakes squealing, it crawled towards the pullout. It was a lumber hauler, pulling a double set of trailers that were stacked only half high on each.

Nico was now hovering in the bushes directly across the road from the pullout and the train-length lumber truck, and he crouched down and gathered up a large smooth stone and a few smaller ones, and waited for his moment.

The truck driver climbed down from the cab and walked around the sides of his flatbed and stopped to look at every wheel set and listen to the hissing hot brakes. They were baking from coming down the steep twisting road, even though he'd been using the low gear and he only had half a load of milled lumber. He leaned against the second trailer and pulled out a cigarette and turned his back to the wind to light it. When the smoke cleared from his face after the first deep drag, he noticed the little shrine across the road; then he saw the dirty ghost of a man standing in the bushes directly behind it, staring at him.

"What the hell are you looking at?" he said, startled by the sight of Nico.

The ghostly figure just stood there, silently watching.

"You're the crazy bastard who crashed his car, aren't you?" the driver yelled.

"That's him, Nico," he heard Marie whisper.

"Are you sure, Marie?" Nico said.

"He's the one," she said. "Kill him, Nico. Kill him for me."

In that instant, Nico's silent gaze changed from patiently studying his target to a monster fueled with flaming hatred. He jumped onto the roadway and hurled the large stone with every ounce of his strength. It sailed through the air and whistled past the driver's mouth, ripping the cigarette from his lips, then smashed into the stacked lumber behind him, sending chips and splinters flying. An instant later, a second smaller stone struck him in the left hip, and he felt a streak of pain running all the way down to his knee. His leg buckled underneath him, but he caught himself before hitting the ground, and now a look of panic flashed across his face. He was about to be struck down by a mad man.

Nico reached for another stone and stepped farther

out onto the asphalt when the piercing scream of an air horn shattered his concentration. He stepped backwards just as a truck hauling long stacks of petroleum drilling pipe came barreling past him and cut off his attack. He watched two more vehicles come past, then he launched himself through the gauntlet of traffic to get to the other side.

The terrified lumber truck driver bolted and leapt into the cab of his truck, which was still idling in neutral, and he jammed it into gear, revved the engine, and dropped the clutch so suddenly that the truck jerked forward with a loud 'bang' as the connecting hitches pulled tight. It was so violent a takeoff that the load of lumber shifted to the rear and snapped the furthest tie-down strap, and a stack of large flat pieces and posts of freshly milled *quebracho* wood came tumbling off the side.

The churning truck wheels in the gravel spun a boiling cloud of dust into the air, and it hung like a morning fog over the river for the longest time. Nico was standing in the middle of it, choking and wiping the sand from his eyes, then a stray gust of wind grabbed the cloud and scattered it to the sky.

When he opened his eyes again, he saw the sections of deep crimson colored quebracho wood laying at his feet, and just as quickly as his mind had fallen into the violent rage at the sight of the truck driver, he was instantly somewhere else.

It was as if he had suddenly awakened standing in

his father's little back alley workshop now, looking at a nicely marbled piece of wood that would soon be made into a garden bench for the most beautiful woman he had ever seen. He could see his father, Gerard, as clear as day as he measured the flat pieces with a tape and marked them with a straight edge for cutting. And he could see the inside of the alley shop, with cutting and sanding tools and a mechanical table top saw that they bought after the shop started to make a little money. He watched as Gerard dampened a shop rag and wiped it across the surface of the wood and the grain and color leapt to the eye, and he turned to Nico and smiled and nodded his head in approval.

"FATHER, today I met the girl I'm going to marry," he said as he came running into the shop. His father was kneeling over and meticulously sanding the curved leg of what would be an elegant desk for a young city councilman. He looked up at Nico and peered over his glasses into his son's eyes, and it struck him perhaps as strongly as Marie's smile had struck Nico. He could see the grip of love awash in them, glinting and shining as never before.

Nico was a strikingly handsome young man in his early twenties, with dark wavy hair and a lean, bronzed physique, and he had many beautiful young girls that caught his eye from one day to the next. But this was different. This one had carved an impression on him unlike any other.

"Tell me about my future daughter then," he said in Italian, as he still used his native language with Nico when it was just the two of them alone. "What's her name?"

"Marie."

"Where does Marie live?" Gerard asked.

"I don't know."

"Well, why is she different than all your other girl friends?"

"I don't know. I mean, I can't explain it. She's just different."

"You don't know why she's different but you're ready to marry her?"

"Yes."

"So where did you meet this girl?"

"At the Botanical Gardens. She sat on the bench you made. And she smiled at me. And I thought I was going to throw up."

"That's it. That's the sign," Gerard said with a laugh.

Nico told his father about how elegantly Marie had sat on the bench, lighting on the seat as gently as a butterfly. He described her as a young farm boy might describe a rare encounter with a royal princess, in awe of her grace and beauty. Then he told him that she asked him to make a very special bench for her private garden. It would be his one and only opportunity to impress her; to show her that he could give her something extraordinary that no one else could.

"It's just a garden bench, Nico. Not a fortune in jewels," Gerard said. But Nico was convinced that with this one small thing he could win her heart, and he would spend the rest of eternity becoming the man she wanted him to be.

Gerard set about the work of crafting a truly unique piece of furniture that would be fit for a princess, much the way he had done so many years ago when he toiled for months on a bamboo fly rod for the Belgian prince. He prayed that Nico would have more success from this labor than he had.

HIS EYES LIT up at the sight of the wood piled in the dirt in front of him, and he couldn't wait to tell her.

"Marie, look what I found!" he yelled. "These will make wonderful benches for our garden!"

Nico spent the next two hours carrying and dragging the heavy pieces of milled quebracho across the hills to his home-camp, one at a time. Quebracho is gruesomely heavy and dense, like a wood laden with iron, and he could feel the weight of it grinding the muscle tissue and bruising the bones as he balanced even the smallest pieces up on his shoulder to carry them back to his camp. When his shoulders were so tender to the touch that he couldn't stand anymore, he continued on by gripping them under his arms and holding them at his hips, and dragging them through the sand, stopping every one hundred yards or so when his hands and arms would go numb from blood loss.

When he had them all there, he started the process of calculating the perfect length and height for two magnificent garden benches, and used a piece of string to measure them to the same precise length, and marked them with the blade of his camp knife. He spent the next two days working almost entirely on the benches; cutting, carving joints in the bases, and fitting them together with hand tools that he pulled from the tool kit in the trunk of the Mercedes, and a large rock for a chisel hammer in a fashion that would have made his father proud.

When they were done, he positioned one close to the fire pit, where he and Marie could spend the evenings sitting together close to the warm fire and gazing at the stars, as she loved to do. The second, he placed on the other side of the pit but a little farther away, and with a view to the river, where he could sit in the mornings and late afternoons with Cristian, watching the trout rise to the early and late hatches of insects, and planning their fishing strategy.

He stood and admired his creations and felt the pride that a man feels when he's done something personal, and special for someone he loves. He bent over and pushed down with all his weight a few times on the bench near the fire pit.

"It doesn't move an inch, Marie!" he said. "The sky will be clear tonight, and we can sit out under the stars for as long as you want."

When darkness fell on home-camp that night, Nico had a fire burning high to fend off the cold air. In the autumn, the days can be warm, but the very instant the sun drops below the mountain tops the temperature plummets, and tonight was going to be a cold night. He opened and cooked the last can of ravioli from Jorge's cache, and listlessly ate the bland little mushy squares, but half he put down for the ants because it left a bitter, metallic numbness on the end of his tongue. He sat on Marie's bench and listened for her voice, but tonight he heard only the crackling of coals and popping of seasoned wood from the fire.

A WEEK HAD PASSED PEACEFULLY since the day Nico found the scraps of wood that now adorned his home-camp. When he sat on the benches to cook or eat, or gaze at the river and the mountains to the west, or to watch the stars drifting over camp in the night, he felt closer to Marie and Cristian, as if they were mediums helping him see through the boundary between this world and the other.

He fished the early morning and late evening hours along the river, moving farther upstream nearly every day to find new pools and riffles and eddies that held trout, and to avoid the channel that passed below the willows where the demon lived in the deep green pool. When he returned each day he came by the highway to check the shrine for offerings from the bus drivers, and occasionally he would torment a truck driver who might stop at the bottom of the hill, if they fit the model he was honing in on.

He was becoming a ghostly legend in the region now. The truck drivers all passed word among themselves at the fuel stations about the crazy bastard that lived in the desert by the river who would attack them at the bottom of the hill. And the bus drivers all felt compelled to stop and place food or little bottles of wine in the shrine, to appease the travel saints and keep Nico from turning on them too.

Even the gauchos and simple people living in the campo in the area avoided this section of highway and the river bottom, believing that a man who was "touched", and might be protected by evil spirits, was living there.

The fact that he survived a car crash as violent as the one that claimed Marie and Cristian, with only a few scrapes, led the locals to believe he was something other than a normal mortal. They didn't quite know what he was, but they feared him just the same.

The only one that didn't seem to be afraid was Pablito, and maybe that was because he saw him immediately after the crash, and he was coming back now on a regular basis and Nico was accustomed to his presence. They shared mate and a fish or fresh baked biscuits almost weekly, and spoke a little more frequently now, despite the fact that Nico had little to say to people who were still in the living world, and Pablito didn't have much to say about anything.

On this particular day, Nico went very far upstream, almost to the head of the valley where the Limay was joined by the Alicura River, in search of new water and just to stretch his legs a bit further. It was almost noon when he came back to home-camp and passed by the shrine.

He stalked up slowly to the road from the opposite side of the shrine this time, and as he crested the hill he saw a small white Chevrolet parked off the edge of the road next to it. He approached it cautiously, and walked around the car and peered in the windows, but it was empty save for a folded map on the passenger seat and a mate thermos on the floorboard.

He looked across the hills to the east to home-camp, and saw a spiraling column of white smoke coming from the fire pit. There was only one person stupid enough to walk into his camp and build a fire during the middle of the day. It had to be Jorge.

"I told you I don't want you here," he said, as he walked into the camp.

"That was almost a month ago. I thought you would be over that by now," Jorge said, as he lifted the lid on the pot of water he was boiling over the fire. He had stacked a box of food and supplies, and even some fishing gear for Nico next to the tent.

"The answer is still no. You can't make me leave," Nico said.

"Who said anything about leaving? And stop being such an asshole. I'm still your friend, whether you want me to be or not," Jorge said. "Listen to me. First, I've been getting calls from the Gendarmerie. The truck drivers you've been throwing stones at have filed reports. If it happens again, they'll come drag your ass out of here and lock you up in a mental institution in Neuquen. Do you understand that?"

Nico stared at him with a hate-filled silence, but slowly nodded his head, as his mind was fully present at the moment. Something was different about Jorge now. The near permanent smile he wore on his face had disappeared, and he looked serious and foreboding.

"Second, I need to let you know that the board of your company has legally removed you, and assigned me as the acting chairman."

"You think I care about that?" Nico said calmly.

"Nico, it doesn't matter what you think anymore," Jorge said almost under his breath, but loud enough to be heard.

Now Nico went into a rage, "You're taking it for yourself, aren't you? You always wanted everything I had. My money, my wife, everything! You've been jealous your whole life!"

Jorge's temper flared back. "Damn it, Nico, I'm the

only one who's trying to protect you! And besides, you wouldn't even have all this money if you hadn't married Marie. Her father is the one who pressured everyone to accept you and do business with you. And now Jacques is coming after you! Do you understand that? He wants to destroy you!"

Nico lunged at Jorge, but his head snapped backwards from a straight left punch that he never saw coming. He was stunned for a second, and his eyes watered up from the blow to his nose, but he charged back at his friend, swinging wildly with both hands. Jorge stepped backward to avoid the fists coming from every direction and grabbed Nico by his shirt and his left arm Then, his foot caught hold of something and they both fell to the ground, with Nico landing on top of Jorge. When they went down, Jorge's back and elbows hit first, then Nico's body came down with all its weight onto Jorge's left hand. He could hear the crushing sound as the bones in his left wrist crumbled and his hand folded back over the top of his forearm. A searing pain shot through his arm to the elbow.

Jorge flailed and kicked himself out from under Nico, and got to his feet.

"You broke my arm, you bastard!" he screamed. Then he wheeled around and ran for the safety of his car.

"If you ever come back here, I'll finish you!" Nico yelled as Jorge fled.

He stood and watched as Jorge stumbled through

the trail to the road, then got in his car and sped away in a fury. When the flush of violence ebbed from his blood, and his clear head returned, he pondered the consequences of the encounter. Maybe Jorge would go straight to the Gendarmerie, and they would come back to arrest him. Or maybe he would find some other way to get back at him.

One thing for certain, everything he had worked his whole life for would probably be gone now. Jorge would see to that. The few things he possessed in this little squat of a camp were all that he would ever have.

He sat on Cristian's wood bench and looked to the western sky, and felt even more alone than he had the first day after the crash.

"I don't deserve anything more. I killed my wife and son because I was a jerk; and now I ran off the only true friend I ever had in my life," he said to himself.

He felt the warm metallic taste in the corner of his mouth, and realized his face was covered with blood. He couldn't tell if his nose was broken, but Jorge had jammed it pretty good, and it was streaming blood. He turned over and laid down on the bench and put his head back to stop the hemorrhaging, and drew his arm up over his eyes to shield them from the burning sun.

"I guess I had that coming," he said to himself. "Marie, did I deserve that?" She was giving him the silent treatment now, so he assumed the answer was yes. His mind was reeling now, thinking about what Jorge said to him. Was Jorge right? Did he make it big only because he married Marie, and her father opened doors for him?

He'd worked every day of his life to pull himself out of the alley that his father's lack of ambition landed him in as a boy. He worked and scraped and plotted his way to a higher life and proved he could achieve anything. He never faltered in his belief in himself, and yet, the instant Jorge challenged that belief he couldn't respond. He had no evidence to bolster his bravado. It was the last remaining bit of his ego being crushed that sent him into the rage.

Maybe he had been a failure at everything in his life, he thought. Business, fatherhood, husband, friend, he doubted every part of his existence. But he made a lot of money and owned property. That was a testament to his worthiness, right?

Marie came from a world and a social class that Nico had never fully been able to understand, but he desired it more than anything else. His greatest mistake was believing that wealth would make him a part of that world. That it would fundamentally change him into someone else. He knew what it was like to be hungry. To wear clothes until they withered and fell from his body. To collect the scraps and trash from other people's lives and view it as a treasure. He saw money as the only barrier between what they were, and what he was not.

He worked, he sacrificed, and he did things that went against his honest nature to be successful; but no matter how much money he made and how many fine things he bought, he was always known as the son of the Italian carpenter. He loved his father, but he never saw the nobility in his character and his strength of perseverance, and in the end it was only the stature of Marie's family ties that brought respect to his name and his money.

He also didn't understand that Marie never really cared. She would have married him regardless, because what she desired most was a life free of the boundaries and obligations of her social class. She wanted to be free to marry a man she loved and admired. His greatest accomplishment in life, was being the man that Marie fell madly in love with. Marie could see past the facade of class, and into the deepest realm of a man's core. And she saw something in Nico that he still didn't see in himself.

JORGE DROVE in agony for an hour, with his left arm collapsed across his lap and the hand still twisted in an unnatural position over the forearm. He was so angry with Nico he could choke the life out of him, but he had to control his anger and the throbbing pain in his arm, and think clearly now. There were plans in motion. Plans within plans; and Nico's reaction had just triggered a new sequence of events. He was prepared for this, in fact he expected it, except the broken bones of course, but that was just a minor distraction. There were fortunes at stake, and lives on the line now, and he had to be deliberate and fully committed with his next moves.

He reached Piedra del Aguila, and luckily already knew where the clinic was located for medical help. They confirmed the obvious, his wrist was broken; but they didn't have any advance scanning or x-ray equipment so they couldn't be sure how many bones were affected or if there was more damage.

They realigned his hand by placing him on a table and while the nurse held his elbow down, the doctor snapped his hand forward. It hurt like bloody hell, and Jorge screamed at the top of his lungs. Then they splinted it with a steel brace and wrapped it tightly with an elastic bandage that would hold everything in place until he could get it X-ray'd. They gave him something to help with the pain, and said he needed to get to a better equipped hospital very quickly before it swelled, and he may need surgery to make sure the bones would knit properly back together.

Jorge decided to drive himself to the hospital in Neuquen, but before he left, he asked if he could use the telephone in the doctor's office, and he made a call to the provincial colonel of the Gendarmerie. His side of the conversation went something like this:

"Colonel Lopez. Thank you for accepting my call."...

"Yes, sir. I did see him, and it went the way you said it would. Badly."...

"I believe it might require the other measures we spoke about yesterday."...

"Are you certain you can supply the men we need for this job?"...

"Yes. I can handle that part of things through my contacts in Buenos Aires, but I may need your support to keep things clean and tidy here on this end. There's a lot at stake if we aren't clever about what we do next."...

At The Feet Of God

Over time, the rusting steel wreckage lost any remaining hints of its fine German heritage and any remnants of wax and shine were burnished away by the sun and the wind-driven sand. But it rested in a peaceful place, with the peaks rising from the Andes and the extinct volcano, Lanin, as a powerful backdrop.

This was the threshold between the arid desert mesa and the land of rivers and mountains that always heralded a sense of homecoming to Marie and Cristian on their yearly passage. The excitement and anticipation of finally reaching Patagonia would fill the car, and every new curve in the road revealed canyons, emerald green water, and sometimes flamingos glowing with pink plumage from sipping the brine shrimp from the shallows.

They would cross the rickety single lane bridge across Rinconada, and when they reached the condor rookery they would know they had arrived. A massive towering vertical rock face, stucco'd white from the dung of a thousand generations of Andean condors raising their young on the narrow ledges. The religious heretic, Charles Darwin, was the first English speaker to see this place and write about it in his journals during his cross-country trek to the Pacific and on to the Galapagos where his infamy would be cemented in history.

Now summer was easing to its end and the poplar trees planted along the arroyo for wind deflection by the first French settlers glowed golden in the early morning light. Venus floated above the eastern horizon in the waning moments of darkness and mimicked the last bright star until the sun crested and erased it from the sky, and the final coolness of the night left a glimmering frost on the rocks and shrubs.

Nico squinted into the orange sunrise and wondered if the world still retained its beauty and color when it was shrouded in darkness. Perhaps darkness is an imaginary condition that only exists in the hearts of tortured men, for he could remember nothing but darkness for the previous months. The few memories of light in his world were fading.

It's a struggle faced by everyone. We dwell on the darkness and it swallows up the moments of joy and buries them deep.

As he looked at the mountains in the west, he suddenly recalled a promise made several years ago. A promise to Marie that one day he would go with her to the top of one of these mountains. She had made the trip herself a few times with local guides, and begged him to go, but he always seemed to be busy or had something to do that held him fast to the city.

"I think today I will climb to the top of that rocky mountain," he said to himself, as he spied a single peak to the west. "Marie loved the views of the Andes from the high country, and I never went with her. I should see it with her, at least once in my life."

He first went about his regular morning routine of building a fire and boiling water to make coffee. He gathered small twigs and mosses to light with a match, then slowly stacked larger dried limbs and branches atop as the fire gained strength.

He was easily snapping and breaking larger branches with just his hands now, or cracking the bigger ones smartly over his thigh with a swift thrust down against his rising leg. He hadn't been badly out of shape when his trip was cut short by the accident, in fact he was considered fairly fit for a city dweller who made his living in an office and spending a large portion of his days riding in the comfortable seat of a German car as he traveled back and forth to meetings with bankers and clients, and suppliers and such.

But the last few months of living such a basic existence in harsh weather with few implements, no conveniences, and a diet consisting largely of fresh fish and charitable handouts had molded him into a different man, at least physically.

Wading every day in swift current and balancing over slippery rocks in the river bottom had carved his lower legs into sinuous foundations, with slender muscles popping from the front of his shins and calves that were cleanly bulging from the opposite side. His upper legs now more resembled tightly wound steel springs with a thin veil of skin and vein overlay from the daily walking and climbing in the steep rocky hills, and his torso had lost all remnants of city-born baby fat, revealing lean ripples of abdominals in the front and intercostal muscles flexing between his clearly visible rib cage.

Even what seemed as an effortless motion of casting a featherlight fly rod for several hours every day had changed his upper body. His shoulders and back were broader and lean, his forearms were thick and bulging, and he had crushing grip strength in his casting hand.

His hands in general had probably suffered the worst during the first weeks and months of survivalist living because they had been used for very little on a daily basis before the accident except for signing papers, shaking hands, holding wine glasses, and caressing a woman's smooth skin. They were fine and soft with neatly groomed and filed nails, and he was obsessive about washing them. He must have washed his hands twenty times a day.

When he was a boy growing up in the back streets,

they were stronger than when he reached his thirties as a man. Here on the river bank, his hands were his principle tool for survival. They were ground with dirt and sand that peeled layer after layer of skin, and the nails became chipped and blood-blackened from smashing them as he labored, and even casting a fly rod in the early days produced an unending array of blisters in the palm and thumb that burst and bled and throbbed late at night. Now in the closing months of summer they were starting to look like Pablito's hands. Swollen thick fingers with girth nearly the same as length, and calloused palms, and skin that was more akin to dried and cracked leather, aged in the baking sun.

His feet had taken a pretty good beating as well, considering he was still wearing the soft traveling shoes that weren't designed with hiking and wading in mind. Although they toughened up quickly after the initial blisters on his heels and big toes healed over.

The deep gash on his left forearm had never completely healed. The infected tissue lingered and once a month or so it would ache and yellow pus would ooze from the scab. It was his constant reminder of the fact he had been flung out of the spinning Mercedes and spared from dying along with Marie and Cristian. It was the physical manifestation of his un-healing guilt.

The mountain he had in mind to climb today was a two hour walk across the highway and over three rolling hills of scrub and thorn. Or, he could walk along the edge of the winding river more easily, then cut straight up the mountain face. It would be a longer trek but more enjoyable he thought, and he might have a chance to scout more fishing holes along the way.

He would travel light, leaving his rod and gear in home-camp and fish the evening hatch for his supper when he got back. The mountain was on the opposite side of the river from the condor rookery, and he imagined he could see for a hundred miles in all directions from the top, if he made it that far.

The river level had fallen low in recent weeks with hotter weather and little rainfall, and it made for easier walking along the flat shore that was covered by water most of the year, but now was a firm bed of black volcanic sand. He reached the base of the mountain and looked up, and felt a wave of utter intimidation wash over him. It was steep and jagged and not nearly as simple a task as he had in his mind when he conceived of doing it; but he turned uphill nonetheless and started his climb.

The driving shoes he was still wearing from the past few months were nearly worn bald on the soles, but the uppers were still serviceable, and they were actually more comfortable now than any pair of shoes he had ever worn. As long as he didn't over-commit his weight on a slippery surface he'd be fine.

He discovered after the first hour, that all the walking he thought had prepared him for this, hadn't in the least. His thighs and ankles were burning from the vertical ascent, and the farther up he went, the more frequently he had to stop and rest his legs and let his lungs catch a breath. The climb up often had him slipping and backsliding down loose rock and pulling himself up by clinging to scrubby plants and small trees that had taken a foothold in the cracks.

Progress was slow and often agonizing, and when he looked back down the mountain he realized there wasn't much of anything to stop him from going all the way to the bottom if his feet came out from under him. He felt like quitting no less than ten times before he reached the midway point on the mountain, and would have likely done just that were it not for an unexpected and thoroughly incredible find.

He was slowly navigating his way up a loose rain trough of gravel, when he lost his footing and smacked his elbow down hard on a large stone. He regained his balance and sat on the stone for safety and cursed and whined at the bleeding and torn skin that peeled away in the impact. Then he noticed what appeared to be more large flat stones placed here and there, almost like steps on a ladder.

He looked farther up the trough and could see the dark outline of what looked like a cave, mostly hidden from view by an ancient cypress tree growing directly out of a massive crack in the rock. It was as if the tree had won a long and hard fought battle, and split the boulder apart for a place to call home.

With his strength and vigor renewed by the

unexpected, he pressed on up the face until he reached the opening, and leaned his head in slowly to let his eyes adjust to the darkness. A part of him feared there might be a puma or some other wild animal living inside, so he was cautious about just walking in, but when he could see well enough he stepped into the darkened room and was mesmerized by what he found.

The opening on the outer face of the rock was the dimension of a small doorway, and he crouched slightly at the waist to clear under it, but once inside, the cave seemed more a cathedral. Almost a perfect circle, about thirty feet in diameter, with a ceiling that was nearly as tall in a gigantic arch. In the upper part of the ceiling facing to the east, a crack allowed a slender sheet of sunlight to enter, and it moved gently across the floor as the sun glided overhead.

The sand floor was so fine it squeaked underfoot as he walked, and the ceiling rock was blackened with the soot of untold thousands of years of campfires. Petroglyphs of creatures that resembled guanacos, painted with the stain of high-mountain berries and nearly faded to the point of being only shadows, surrounded the inner walls around the opening, and the painted outlines of human hands of all sizes, hundreds of them, adorned the other areas of the interior stone.

He felt the sudden impression of being an intruder in someone else's home, even though this cave had probably not been used for hundreds or thousands of years, but it still made him feel uncomfortable.

He could see the remnants of small stone tools, and a large boulder that stood in the center that was probably flat at some time, but had been worn into a deep basin in the middle over the centuries of people using it to grind plants or grains or other things in the center of it. And laying atop the grinding rock was a single piece of shiny black basalt, chipped into a razor edged spear point, with the tip still as sharp as a needle, as if it had just been finished and was laid ready to be tied to the end of a weapon, but abandoned in haste by its maker.

On the ground near the entrance was the tattered remains of fine leather straps that had decayed or been gnawed upon by rodents over the score of time, and a cluster of three odd little piles of small round stones.

SEVEN THOUSAND YEARS BEFORE, give or take a few hundred years, a young boy stood there in the same entrance way of the cave, and stared out across the hillside and the lush green valley below, and down to the river that measured nearly three miles to the far side in those days.

It was like a slender sea that moved across the pampas and splintered out to the eastern ocean in a series of inland rivers. He held in his hands the most efficient hunting weapon his father owned, a Bola. Made from thinly sliced strips of tanned leather that were braided into strong rope; there were three, each about a yard in length that neatly spliced together in the center. On the ends of each rope was attached a leather sack, tightly filled with round stones and sewn shut with sinew pulled into thread from dried gut.

This cave was the summer home his clan had used for an infinite number of generations. None of them could remember a story of any of their clan ever spending a summer anywhere else but in this cave, and the hand signatures of each clan member who ever existed covered the inside like modern wallpaper, including the seven who lived there now. It was a personal record of their family back to the first days of the Tehuelche, the "Fierce People".

The Tehuelche spent the summer and fall months higher in the Andes, in caves like this one if they were lucky enough to find them, hunting game animals and stocking up on the tools and clothing and supplies needed for survival. In the winter months they migrated back to the temperate valleys of the smaller rivers and streams, and caught fish and crabs and shore birds, and lived in small huts made from the pelts of guanacos. They were nomads, traveling light and living from day to day in a land that was plentiful and generous.

The boy was called K'achorro by his people, and he was growing in the image of his father, tall with a slender and muscular build, large dark eyes set widely apart, and coarse long hair as black as the night. His father stood nearly six feet ten inches, which was considered tall even for the Tehuelches, but they were a race of giants compared to other native cultures around the world.

Today would have been the day his father taught him to become a boleadoro, and to hunt with the weapon that fed his clan. This area of the Andean range was thick with guanacos, which was their primary source of food and clothing and tools at this time of year. Meat, fine bones for weapons and needles, points for fishing spears, leather for bolas and skins for clothing and huts.

The rheas, which are cousins to the ostrich, were also plentiful here and always found near the guanacos because they frequently fed from their dung. Their eggs were a delicacy and the meat was rich with nutrients and fat, like the great fish that came into the rivers to breed in the fall before they started their migration.

The bola was the perfect hunting weapon for the long-legged creatures of the Patagonian pampas, and becoming an expert with it ensured the survival of the entire clan. It was swung overhead and launched with force and momentum, and in the hands of a skilled hunter it would entangle the legs of the big animals and bring them quickly to the ground, where the hunters would then pounce and cleanly cut their throats with an obsidian blade, or thrust a basalt tipped spear into the heart for a speedy kill.

No one could remember who made the first bola or where the idea came from, nor how they learned to use it, but it was a weapon that connected many cultures all over the planet, much like the pyramids that once dotted the landscapes on every continent with no concrete recollection of who built them, or how. The Aleuts and Inuits on the other side of the world in the Arctic were using precisely the same weapon to hunt the vast flocks of sea ducks along the freezing coastline from their walrus skinned kayaks; flinging the bola into the ducks as they passed overhead and entangling their wings.

K'achorro stood at the entrance running the leather straps through his fingers and getting a feel for the weighted ropes, and imagining his twirling throw and release, when the flush of birds and flutter of wings passing in front of the doorway caught his attention.

He put his father's bola down beside the door and stepped outside into the morning light and saw the covey of birds still flushing in waves from the thick cover below the cave, and one passed directly in front of his face and dropped a small cypress cone at his feet. He knelt down and held the cone in his hands, and for no particular reason, he dug a shallow trench in the sandy crack of rock in front of the cave, and buried it for safe keeping.

He never heard or saw the giant cat coming. Nearly invisible among the rocks and briars, he was over six hundred pounds of muscle and meanness, with front teeth like ten inch scythes with only one purpose, instant death. The feline came in a low rush, moving like a bolt of tawny colored lightning, and knocked K'achorro flat to his back. Then it seized him by the throat, driving the dagger-like teeth in one side and cleanly out the other, and breaking his neck in a swift crushing clench of his jaws.

His father had been standing in the center of the cave working at his rock alter on a new spear point when he looked up and saw the long saber toothed-cat standing and holding K'achorro's lifeless body by the neck like a small weightless creature. It stared back at him with huge golden eyes, and curled its upper lip and uttered a throbbing guttural growl without releasing the boy. A combination of startled fear and disbelief at what he was seeing caused K'achorro's father to scream in a high pitched wail that reverberated through the cave and brought the entire clan instantly to their feet.

The big cat spun and disappeared down the trail with K'achorro in his grip, and the clan grabbed what they had close at hand and pursued him down the mountain, but he would never be seen again. After that day, the cave became a cursed place in the minds of the elders, and they would never return again to their ancestral summer home.

NICO COULD SEE the beauty of this cave as a protective dwelling, but he wondered about why the ancients might have chosen to live so high on the mountain and have to endure the arduous climb every day. Maybe it was safer from predators or other clans; or maybe in those times the river was more like an ocean and not so far down from the cave as now, he thought. The temperature inside the cave felt amazingly cool despite the burning heat outside, and the crack in the ceiling allowed for a gentle breeze of fresh air to be pulled in through the doorway and upward.

Nico sat just inside the doorway in the shade for a long time, resting and looking out over the valley and the river below. It would have been an easy thing to call this his victory and go no further, but he had committed in his mind to reach the top of this mountain, and he made an oath to Marie, so onward he went.

In just half an hour more, he reached the summit; exhausted, but feeling a sense of having fulfilled his promise. He was seeing the mountains for the first time from the eagle's view. The view that Marie had told him about so many times, and he had smiled and feigned interest, but couldn't really understand her emotional reaction.

He sat on a rock that jutted out over the ledge, and let his legs hang freely with two thousand feet of air beneath them. The air at this altitude was thin and forced him to breath more rapidly, but the vista took his mind completely away from his burning lungs and for a few moments, away from so many other things.

From the eagle's perch, the river valley below appeared vastly different, lacking the distraction of detail and seeming in the same instant as an enormous living landscape that shifted and swayed with the rhythm of wind as it grazed the earth, and clouds and sky that rotated above towards a different destination.

Up close at river's edge, the waves of the river rolled and crashed and sprayed, and the flittering of wings and leaves, and dust and raindrops and all manner of small living things draw the eyes quickly here and there. But from above, the river looked like a large sheet of textured silk fabric sprinkled with sparkling stardust, and being drawn by some magical force across the land. The surrounding shapes of earth and mountain shifted gently between shadow and light, being painted by a curtain of clouds that shielded or shone the rays of the sun.

To the west, the towering volcano, Lanin, stood clearly in his face. It was a massive inverted cone with a glacier cap, and it was so tall that it made its own weather at the top with clouds and snow or wind racing around the peak and fading or growing thicker with the moisture coming from the Pacific Ocean.

The big rivers, the Chimehuin and the Collon Cura flowed down from the Andes and joined the Limay, and the beautiful green Caleufu twisted through the tall peaks and joined them in a wide valley. Nico's timberland lay just on the other side of the mountain where the Caleufu was born in a giant cascading waterfall where the two smaller streams, the Filo Hua Hum and the Meliquina joined hands and ran together.

He heard many times from the gauchos who lived near the timberland that the Caleufu had brown trout the size of tree trunks in it, but it could only be explored in the spring time when the water was deep enough to float with a raft, and it was perilous going. It wasn't a trip for the faint of heart, but one day a man might dare to run it and challenge the river-gods with a fly rod.

The only living things with a more celestial view than Nico were the family of condors, an adult pair with three juveniles, soaring over the thermal lift zone between the rugged mountain peak and the valley. The adults were easy to spot with their thick white furry collars wrapped around their long necks, and they were holding school for the youngsters in the way of using thermal lifts to stay aloft with nary a single beat of their twelve foot wing span. The five of them spun in a circle, one behind the other, and as the clouds would pass over the rising air and instantly cool it, they would slowly sink in altitude until the rays of sun hit them again and lifted them higher to the heavens.

He sat there for a long time watching the family soaring together and pondered all the things he and Marie would never be able to do with Cristian. He would never see him finish school and become the first man of the Azzarà clan to go to university and graduate with honors in some professional discipline like he'd always dreamed. He would never see him leave home and seek his own destiny and raise his own family. He would never see him soar in his own sky.

He felt sadness here, but he felt sad everywhere. There wasn't any escaping the sadness, but it was different here on this mountain top. It took nearly all his strength and concentration to reach this place without getting killed, so when he fell into the memories, and grips of guilt for promises never kept or things never done, they didn't carry the same heavy weight on his shoulders. They were lighter somehow, and when it came time to begin his descent, the sadness would leave him in peace for his journey. The climb and the descent, just as the time he spent wading in the river in search of trout, brought long moments of cessation during which he could lay down the burden of sadness for at least a little while.

The other thing, that he didn't realize yet, was that here on this mountain top at the edge of the clouds and the feet of God, he was nearly always able to remember Marie in her happier moments. Those gentle memories that made him smile and laugh and feel the slightest hint of warmth glowing in his heart. He knew she would have loved being here with him. She would have loved the idea that he was coming here, even without her.

As much as he wanted to hear her voice and not let her go from his sight, when he sat in the evenings by the fire at home-camp, with the crumpled remains of the Mercedes only feet away, their conversations were often brooding and serious. They left him feeling heavy and burdened as he lay down to sleep every night. But this was a place of healing.

He would return here several times before the full onset of winter arrived, and again in the earliest days of spring. Sometimes on cloudless clear days when he could see nearly to the Pacific Ocean, and on others he sat above the clouds as they blanketed the valley below the mountain top. And every time he came he grew stronger in his body, and stronger in spirit.

The growling ache in his stomach reminded him that he hadn't eaten yet today, and he knew it might be a longer trip back down the mountain than it was coming up because the loose shale and gravel were treacherous footing. He'd considered from time to time if he might be better off joining his wife and son, but dying alone on this mountain with two broken legs wouldn't be his preference. Although he supposed it would be a beautiful place to go, and the freezing temperatures at night this high would make it an easy passing. Still, he took his time and minded his steps.

An hour into his downward journey, Nico paused and sat on a large rock to catch his breath and watch the cars and trucks inching their way along the twisting road from the high mesa down to the valley floor, then along the winding river heading west and southeast. They looked like ants moving in single file from this distance above, but he could easily distinguish the roadway and the vehicles.

He kept a keen eye on the truck drivers' pullout on

the flat out of habit and he still felt a stinging need for revenge when he would see a log or lumber truck coming, but what he saw next suppressed his anger and raised the hairs on the back of his neck.

A featureless black sedan came down the mountain road at a slow pace and paused for just an instant on the outside edge of corner number seventeen, as if they were inspecting the place where Nico's Mercedes had gone over, then it proceeded to the bottom and eased over into the pullout and parked. No one left the car, no movement, nothing.

"Who are they?" Nico thought to himself.

"What are you looking for?"

"Are you looking for me?"

His mind was immediately awash with paranoia. The death squads of the AAA, the Argentine Anticommunist Alliance, favored cars just like this one. Usually Ford Falcons, in a four door configuration, made especially for the government in the Ford assembly plant in Buenos Aires. He couldn't tell from this distance if, in fact, it was a Ford Falcon, but it looked similar enough to make him panic.

"Jorge. Jorge did this to me," he said out loud.

"What did you tell them about me, Jorge? You lying bastard, what did you tell them about me?"

He imagined Jorge skulking in some secret dark alleyway with trench coated agents of the AAA, and telling them lies about his associations with leftist sympathizers. They might just believe it after all, because Nico was raised in the poor backstreets. It would be a very plausible conclusion.

"But I never did any harm to anyone in my life!" he cried.

"I didn't support the communists. I went fishing with the President for Christ's sake!"

The car sat stopped in the pullout for at least five minutes, then started and turned back onto the highway, and drove back in the direction it came from. Nico stayed in his hiding place high up on the mountain for another hour, just to make sure they weren't coming back, before he continued his slow descent, and he tracked back along the river bank rather than going by the pullout and checking the little shrine to see if a bus driver had left any food.

Just as he was finding the first speck of healing calmness in his life, everyone it seemed was conspiring against him. He wasn't just alone in the world, he was being hunted.

The Gift

The Patagonian skies in summer are among the rarest of natures wonders. The Pacific winds coming all the way from Asia blend with cold air moving north from the Antarctic and form waves of thermal current rolling up and down in the atmosphere like an invisible ocean in the sky. Where these unseen waves peak, the water vapor forms clouds called lenticulars that resemble hovering space ships from some far off galaxy, and as the winds blow east the ships stay perfectly still, balanced on the crest of their wave and never moving. They appear in the sky almost daily in the spring and summer but are seldom seen in other parts of the world.

As summer turns to autumn, the invisible ocean waves in the atmosphere change from a smooth rolling current to stormy seas of air, and when they do the clouds turn to churning masses and reflections from the falling sun cooks them to a caldron of red flaming liquid, boiling over the mountain tops.

It was just such a fiery sky that hovered over Nico in recent afternoons as he was making his hike back to home-camp. The color was mesmerizing, and ominous in the same instant. Since the first day he sighted the black sedan lingering at the turnoff, he had seen it twice more. Always late in the afternoon, and always it remained motionless with no sign of who was inside, or what they were plotting. It was obvious they were watching his home-camp from a safe distance and searching for him, but he was clever and kept himself away from camp late in the day.

He rose with the light and made coffee every morning, then left to hike the river line westward to fish, being sure to keep himself concealed from view of the roadway above. When he returned late in the day, he approached from the high hills with the sun at his back, and carefully surveyed the scene below before crossing into the open to check the shrine for food, then on to home-camp.

He also noticed a number of times, a dark green truck of the Gendarmerie cruising slowly up and down the twisting mountain road, and twice stopping at the curve high above to peer over the edge. Maybe they were in on it too; searching and spying to find Nico, but he didn't care.

Nico remained as fixed to this place as the first day. He felt Marie and Cristian's presence all around him and could see their faces in the landscapes and sunsets and the flowing river. He could hear Marie's voice in the low crackling fire at night under the stars, and he could feel Cristian's small hands gripping the cork handle of the fishing rod beneath his with every cast to the rising trout in the early mornings. They were still with him here, and he was determined to never lose them again.

After the fight with Jorge, Nico discovered a small treasure of luxuries in a large cardboard box inside the tent, with a flashlight and batteries, and some canned food and bags of fresh mate, and a box of well tied fishing flies. There was even a bottle of Irish whiskey that Jorge brought along for sipping by the fire at night, but there would be no more visits from Jorge nor resupply of basic necessities. That was over. Nico didn't trust his oldest friend anymore, and thought surely he was up to dastardly deeds.

"Why did you bring all of this to me, Jorge?" he said to himself.

"Did you want me to stay here? Was that it?" he pondered.

"That's the truth of it, isn't it! You wanted me to be comfortable so I would stay here just long enough for you to get control of everything back in Buenos Aires and take it all for yourself!" he screamed out loud. "And now you've got your little spies watching me."

After a long while, his anger over Jorge drifted away because he just didn't care about the life he left behind him in Buenos Aires. Everything he cared about was here. And eventually over time and nothing happening, his obsession with the spies faded. He would see them from time to time, but he never saw them leave their cars.

Most days for company he had the birds that came to wake him at the first hint of sunrise, and the little desert foxes that would sneak in to steal the remainder of his fish dinner, and several times a week now there were bus drivers traveling north from Bariloche who would stop and place a small meal and a candle in the little shrine on the road. He never saw their faces or knew their names, but he appreciated their kindness. They were his true friends now.

He spent his time walking along the river and climbing to the eagle's perch above the cave to sit and think about Marie, gathering driftwood for fires, and fishing. He hadn't realized it until now, but he was also starting to look forward to Pablito's weekly visits.

In the earliest days, Nico felt the weight of being alone but it was almost liberating in many ways. He didn't have to live by obligations or anyone else's needs or plans, and he could just do whatever he felt like doing or do nothing at all, which he did a lot of. But at some point, just being alone grew into loneliness, and when it came, the loneliness felt heavy and dark and it brought the most desperate evil thoughts to his mind.

Pablito never had much to say, but when he did it was meaningful, and he had a deep appreciation for even the smallest elements of his life. He had lived most of his life with so little compared to Nico, and yet, he had lived every day being grateful for what he had, and Nico had lived with a constant hunger for more. Small flecks of the gratitude were starting to rub off on Nico now.

One morning in April, Nico woke to find the first heavy frost covering the ground and the plants around home-camp, and the sides of the flimsy tent were crusty and hard. He'd managed to pry open the trunk of the car long before to recover the bags of luggage they packed for the summer trip, and he had a couple of light sweaters for the cool nights, but he'd been living in a state of mind that existed only in the present, and the coming change of seasons was outside his reckoning. When the bags were packed months ago he wasn't planning on spending a cold winter on the river bank in Patagonia.

When the sun had risen enough to start melting the crystals on the tent and the sand started feeling soft under foot again, Nico walked down to the river and knelt down to wash out his little tin coffee pot and refill it with fresh water, and he looked up to see Pablito coming across the other side. He smiled and waved, and Pablito raised his hand out from under his poncho, then tapped his horse with a heel to encourage him across the cold river in the shallow wide vado.

"Hola, Pablito! I see you brought winter with you today," Nico said.

"No, no, Don Nico. This is just the first sign. The

mountains are starting to turn red now, but in a few weeks they will be white with snow."

"I'm just making fresh coffee, come join me," Nico said.

"*Dale*." Pablito responded, then he slid down from the tall saddle and pulled a rolled bag from the tie loop and carried it with him to the camp.

Nico filled the top of the little pot with fresh coffee grounds and placed it on a wire rack that hung over his fire pit, and they sat on Marie's bench and put their hands out over the fire to warm them.

"Every time I come here you have something new, Don Nico," Pablito said, as he was admiring the bench.

"I found this wood by the roadside and I made this bench for my wife, Marie, and put it here because she loves watching the fire late at night. The other I made for my son, Cristian, so we can sit and watch the river when the fish are rising. I'm teaching him to fish this summer," Nico said, as he hung the coffee pot over the fire.

He stared directly into the flames without ever looking up, as if he needed to concentrate intently to hold onto his vision of Marie and Cristian. If he looked into Pablito's eyes, the fantasy might vanish.

Pablito glanced at him, and he too stared into the flames as if he was seeing the same spirits. Then he took a small stick and poked at the fire to rustle the flames higher. When the coffee pot signaled it was ready with a gurgle and steamy whistle, Pablito said,

"My wife has sent along some gifts for you today, Don Nico."

"I haven't deserved a gift in a long time," Nico said.

"My wife said that you are our neighbor now, and it would please her to do neighborly things for you. Por favor, don't refuse my wife's gifts, or I will not be able to go home tonight!" he said with a laugh.

"Very well, if it keeps you on good terms with your wife, I accept. Let's see what she has sent."

Pablito opened the wool bag and pulled out a paper sack and a small glass jar.

"She was up early this morning baking fresh bread, and she insisted I bring some for breakfast with fresh *rosa mosqueta* marmalade that she canned last week," Pablito said.

"Where did she find the rose hips to make the marmalade?" Nico asked.

"It's all around you, Señor. I'm sure she would make more for you, if you picked some berries for her."

Nico looked around him, and realized for the first time that the hills around his home-camp were engulfed by the thorny wild rose hip bushes, the rosa mosquetas, all full of the bright red berries that swelled after the pink summer flowers had fallen. He couldn't remember seeing either the flowers or the berries around him in all these months, but his mind had spent much of the time dwelling in some other place besides the physical world.

Pablito pulled a thick golden loaf of bread from the paper bag and handed it to Nico, and he tore a large piece from the end and held it near his nose so he could smell the fresh doughy aroma. It even smelled warm on the inside, and it reminded him of bread his mother made back in Italy when he was a boy, long before they boarded the ship that brought them to South America.

He pulled his little tool from his pocket and opened the blade and dipped out some rosa mosqueta and spread it thickly over the soft inside part of the bread, then put it in his mouth and let it roll on his tongue for a second or two before he chewed and swallowed. A little wave of sugary euphoria swept over him.

While Nico was enjoying the bread, Pablito went back to his horse to fetch the second gift from his saddle bag. He came back to the fire pit carrying a neatly folded poncho, and said, "It would honor my wife and me if you would accept this."

Pablito's wife spent most of the summer months working in her spare time to make two or three finely woven and decorated ponchos from llama wool that had been cleaned and dyed by hand, and she sold these each year at the annual gathering of the gauchos and their families, called the *Puestero*. She had not met Nico, but Pablito shared his story with her, and mentioned his visits every time he came by, and she decided a poncho was exactly what a man living in the open campo needed more than anything else. With the first frost of Autumn coming this morning, she couldn't have been more right.

The ponchos worn by gauchos are one of their most

prized possessions, second only to their knives or horses. They are woven so tightly from the course hair of llamas or alpacas that they are almost impenetrable to rain and snow, and even when wet they keep the man wearing it warm and protected from the fierce winds. The designs and colors woven into the fabric are unique to the woman who makes them and the region where they live, and this one was a natural grey with black stripes down the center and the sides, and white scrolling within the stripes.

It represented two months worth of labor by Pablito's wife, and it was a gift of genuine compassion for a man she had never met.

Nico held out his hands and Pablito laid the poncho across his forearms, and he was surprised by the weight. It was heavy and thick, and as soft as a newborn lamb. He put it across his knees and ran his hands across the wool, and he was overcome with emotion.

His mind was searching through years of gifts and fine things he had been given by wealthy people, important people, and yet he couldn't remember ever receiving something so generous and heartfelt from someone he didn't even know. And this person had absolutely nothing to gain from the gift.

He took a second to compose himself, then swallowed hard before looking up at Pablito. His eyes were blinking back the tears and he choked on the words when he tried to open his mouth and speak. Then tried again.

"Thank you my friend," he whispered.

"Please tell your wife, this is the most precious gift anyone has ever given to me."

He stood to keep from having to speak anymore, and unfolded the poncho and pulled it over his head. It draped closely to his body and he could feel the warmth building beneath the wool cover almost instantly. It was more than just a gift of clothing and protection from the harsh Patagonian winter. It was a gift that would keep him here with Marie and Cristian for as long as he wanted.

Pablito finished his breakfast and coffee, and was getting ready to leave and mend a fence line in the upper pastures, when he turned to Nico and said, "I will be through here again in three days to move horses from the upper pasture to the winter pasture on the other side of the river. Come with me."

"On horseback?" Nico said.

"Unless you want to run behind me all the way up the mountain. I will bring a gentle horse for you," Pablito said with a wry smile.

Nico considered the notion for a moment. He had never been on a horse a day in his life, even though Marie begged him constantly every summer when they came to San Martin de los Andes. She loved to ride horses up into the mountains.

"I'll be waiting for you," Nico said.

As he watched Pablito riding back across the river, he turned back to the bench and said, "Did you hear that, Marie? I'm taking you on a horseback ride into the mountains in three days!" She didn't answer, but he didn't care. He smiled at the thought of her watching him ride into the high country, and the new adventure they would talk about over the fire at night.

On this night, the stars and a three-quarter moon dimly lit the landscape, and the river was a sparkling monochrome picture in front of the mountains. Nico left the warm camp fire and moved over to sit for a while on Cristian's bench and gaze at the river in the evening light. The air was crisp now in the darkness, and he pulled his new poncho around him to fend off the cold and enjoy a little more time outside before crawling into the tent.

He could hear a splash or a chase from time to time coming from the water. Life doesn't stop for darkness in the river world, and the creatures there don't sleep like the animals on dry land. They are always vigilant for a meal or an enemy, and on moonlit nights the big fish that lay near the deep rocky bottom can see every little thing above them swimming and flowing with a perfect back light.

He heard a faint rustle from the bushes, and the scurrying little feet across the rocks before he saw the shadowy little animal moving from the safety of thorny cover to the river. He couldn't tell what it was in the darkness, a large rat or a tiny opossum perhaps, but it crept warily down to the river for a drink of cool water, then it waded into the river and swam furiously to reach the other side.

Nico felt the impending attack rising from the back of his mind before it actually happened. He could sense the giant demon fish deep in his lair coming to attention with the change in the river. Something that didn't belong there had entered his realm. Something pitifully slow in the water and sizable for a meal.

The little animal reached the strongest part of the middle current in the river and it washed him downstream, but he kept paddling towards the opposite bank and finally broke free of the swift water and came into the calm only a few feet from the safe shore. Then a moment later he was crawling out of the water onto a rock at the edge, and lifting his head and front legs up into the dry air when the calm water around him erupted. The explosion of water into the night air shone like fluorescent crystals in the moonlight, spraying ten feet upward and hanging for an instant before they showered back to the flow. There was a squeal, a tail slap, and then the silence of the night.

A Blade

Today Nico went farther up river than he'd ever been, past the mountain to the eagle's perch, and at least another two miles. The river widened into a marsh belt that was chocked full of wading birds and iridescent ducks of blue and gold and green, and flamingos that were gliding forward on their thin stalks of legs and skimming the brine from the surface of the shallow water.

The main channel of the river flowed around the outside bend and it was clear and cold, and colder every mile closer to the water's source in the melting snow. The bottom of the river was tiled with stones like a painter's palette, and wading quietly into the water gave the sense of stepping gently into an enormous canvas, painted by a brilliance beyond his understanding.

These were the moments when he ceased trying to

understand, or to qualify or quantify the world around him. The attempt to define everything around him and everything that happened to him was madness here. Here, the elements of the world would tell him who he was, not the other way around. His only purpose was to accept life as it came, and be the man life told him to be.

By now, the way he fished had evolved into the unconscious and ethereal form. He didn't need to think about how to move the rod to make it place the fly where it needed to be, nor even where the fly needed to be. His hands and the motion of his casts moved in rhythm with the elements around him. The rod would bend and load and flow forward, and the line would hiss and sing in the wind and float gently to the surface. And as a fish rose and accepted his fly, he would sense the take before it happened and the reel would spin and spray against the fight before he gained the advantage and brought his dinner to hand.

He only took trout from the river that were a good size to eat for a single meal, and nothing more. The big fish he was normally sending back to the river because he knew that they were the breeding fish that kept the river full, but he usually fished on now after catching his meal because he didn't want the pleasure of being a part of the canvas to end too quickly, and he released the additional fish back to the water unharmed.

He pinched down the barbs on his hooks to keep from

injuring the fish, and stayed in the river until his legs turned purple and scaled with hard bumps. Then he would relent and wade out and begin the long walk back to home-camp. Then he would sit by the fire and tell Marie about his day.

The sun was nearly down below the mountain as he prepared to cross back over the road in view of home-camp. A few cars were traveling south, heading to San Carlos de Bariloche or maybe even farther south to Esquel, and he paused, hidden in the brush, to let them pass before walking over to the little shrine. He found a tightly wrapped paper bag tucked underneath that contained a couple of sandwiches and a package of Oreo cookies, and he felt blessed that a bus driver had stopped and remembered him today, because he kept only a single small rainbow trout from the river for dinner.

He tucked the paper bag under his poncho and looked east to the camp and immediately saw something amiss; the tent was flattened on the ground. Then he saw movement, a man, and now a second, moving quickly around his camp.

"Robbers!"

Nico flew across the rocks and through the brush, covering half a kilometer in what felt like an eternity to him, but probably appeared like mere seconds to anyone who may have witnessed it from the road above. The anger inside him boiled hotter and more murderous with every leap. By the time he crested the final hill, he had summoned the fury of every insult and injury ever suffered in his lifetime.

Every beating he took as a boy in the streets of Buenos Aires, every ounce of resentment he harbored in poverty, and his hatred of the world that had robbed him of his greatest love and child; it was all propelling him forward. He was utterly demonic in form when he came racing down into the camp screaming in a violent, incoherent rage.

The two criminals were caught completely unaware. The one on the far side of the car was older and bald, with a ragged beard and a dirty red scarf tied around his sun-blackened neck. He had used a short steel bar and pried the twisted hood of the Mercedes open and was jerking and cutting lines, hoses and wires with a folding knife to pull out engine parts.

At the sight of the devil busting through the bushes and into the camp, he let out an involuntary shriek, dropped everything in his hands and wheeled and ran directly into the dense prickly michay. Then worse yet, into the dagger-thorn rosa mosqueta bushes, shredding his clothes and bloodying his face and arms. He screamed in agony twice from the thorns tearing at his flesh as he pushed through and up the hill, but he left his compatriot without a second thought and never looked back.

The second was younger, bigger, and had an angry round face enveloped by long greasy hair. He was rifling through the few meager possessions that Nico had in the tent and the canvas duffle bag, and he stood up to see what the commotion was all about just in time to see Nico clearing the opening into the camp about twenty feet away. His hand moved down to a large kitchen knife he had tucked into his waistband, but it was too late. Nico covered the distance like a wounded lion in a full on death charge and unleashed a torrent of violence, smashing him backward into the fire pit.

They both hit the ground, and Nico leaped over on top. He sat up straddling the thief's stomach and drove his fist straight into his chest like a crushing hammer blow, and the air in his lungs burst out his mouth in an explosive, coughing gasp. Then Nico followed it with a flurry of strikes to his cheek bones, and as the criminal tried to turn away from the onslaught of punches, Nico struck him with a fierce downward plunge of his elbow to the left side of his head.

The last blow made him go as limp as a codfish. Nico paused his attack and sat back upright on his chest, when suddenly the villain pulled the knife from his waistband and tried to slash at his neck. But Nico jerked his elbow out in reflex and deflected the strike short, and only the tip of the blade grazed the upper part of his shoulder at the base of his neck.

Nico grabbed the knife wielding hand with his left and gouged his right thumb deep into the villain's eye socket until he wailed in agony, then Nico rolled quickly off of him and got to his feet and out of range of the long knife. The greasy haired thief rolled the other way and came to his feet swinging the blade wildly in front of him and squealing from the pain in his eye.

There was a stream of blood pouring from his nose and his left ear, and his cheek was instantly swelling from a fractured orbital bone and his eye was miserably useless. He backed up two steps and turned and vanished into the falling darkness. Nico could hear his fading whimpering for several minutes as he stumbled through the thorns and navigated his way back up to whatever foul place he came from.

Nico's heart was still racing and the anger that had been lingering inside him for a couple of months was overflowing. The ugly bastard who tried to knife him had unleashed a vengeful wraith, and he was lucky to escape with his life.

A few of his things had been stuffed into the canvas duffle bag, including a wiring harness and a couple of small engine parts and trim pieces from the Mercedes, so they were planing on using his own duffle to carry out things they could steal. Nico was still enraged, but also stunned that these corrupt scum would want to take even more from him.

"I've lost everything! Everything in my life that means anything to me!" he yelled into the night sky.

"Why in the name of God would you want to steal what little I have left!?"

He fell to his knees and slumped forward, and sobbed. He'd only cried once since the accident and that was from bursting rage, but this time the sense of complete and total loss gripped him. He had truly lost everything that meant anything to him, and now he was having to battle to keep the meaningless bits that were left.

For a moment, he thought about his companies and his wealth, and his home in Recoleta and the beautiful house he purchased in San Martin de Los Andes, even though Marie had just wanted a small cottage in the pasture near the pine forest. He thought about everything he had worked so hard to buy. And in that moment he would have traded it all to have Marie and Cristian back in his arms.

The only things that made him a truly wealthy man had been taken from him, only three feet from where he was sitting.

He took a deep breath to calm himself and wiped his eyes with the edge of his poncho, and when his vision cleared the first thing that came into focus, and for some unknown reason seized his attention, was a large stone on the outer ring of the fire pit. It was one that Pablito had gathered and stacked to shield the wind on the day he came to inspect the car wreck, and where he cooked two little trout for breakfast and left the coffee can and matches for Nico.

The stone wasn't round like most of the others that rolled and wore down after thousands of years in the flowing river, but had been broken into a shape almost like a pyramid, with angular sides that came to a point and a flat bottom; and with the embers still glowing from the fire pit, he could see light reflecting in crystals that grew from the inside. It was a remnant of the volcanoes that rimmed this part of the world, and over millions of years the gas bubbles trapped in molten rock boiled and cooled and turned into gems, hidden from sight and waiting to be discovered.

He pulled the stone up from its place around the pit and wiped the dust and dirt from the surface, then placed it in the exact spot in the smooth gravel bank where he'd last glimpsed Marie and Cristian. Then he built a new fire and sat watching the light glistening on the little stone monument like a thousand tiny stars.

Nico kept his camp fire burning through the night and stayed huddled outside in the flickering glow, listening to every slight sound and animals calling in the desert. When the sunrise finally came, he was curled up in the sand and wrapped tightly in the poncho with the smoldering embers just beginning to cool.

PABLITO LEFT his small cabin early again this morning to swing by and pick up Nico on his way to the high pasture where they had fifteen horses grazing in the late-summer sweet grass. There were two new foals born in early spring, and they should be halfway to weaning by now so he wanted to see if they were healthy and the mares still nursing. He came in from the Caleufu River valley this time, and forded the Limay in the wide flat vado where the water level was low all the way across. Then, he followed the shore line up to Nico's camp site.

He thought of Nico as a friend, and as he was living within the area he had responsibility for, he also felt some responsibility for him as if he were a part of the herd that free ranged in the estancia and had to survive the elements largely on his own.

As he came in sight of the camp he saw Nico sitting by the fire pit, and he saw the tent flattened on the ground and also noticed the hood of the Mercedes had been raised. He raised his hand when Nico looked up and saw him, and Nico raised his in turn, but he could tell something bad had happened during the night. He rode straight into home-camp with a second saddled horse ponying behind his big gray for Nico.

"What happened?" he said, as he looked around the scattered remnants of the camp.

"Robbers." Nico said. "They were tearing through my camp last night when I came in, but I bloodied one of them up good."

"Are you hurt?" Pablito asked. He could see the blood stain on Nico's neck and saturated into the shoulder of his poncho.

"A small cut. The bastard tried to stab me, but I bloodied him up. He won't come back here, you can bet on that."

"I better have a look at it," Pablito said, as he dismounted his horse and tied the reins up. He pulled the neck of the poncho back and looked over the cut that ran back to front across the neck muscles that run down to the shoulder. It wasn't deep and it had scabbed over during the night, so he didn't think it needed to be stitched. "Did they take anything important?"

"I don't have anything important," Nico said.

"I'll see where they went," Pablito said. He untied the second horse and lashed its reigns to a bush and swung up fast onto the gray and started criss-crossing up the hill around the thorn bushes looking for tracks. He returned a half hour later with numerous patches of bloody clothing in his pouch.

"They must have had a car parked up on the road high above, and they left in a hurry from there. They didn't want to leave the car on the flat pullout where you could see them coming. It looks like they left their pound of flesh in the rosa mosqueta on the way back too," He said, holding out the blood stained strips of shirts and pants with a hint of a smile. "You don't have to ride with me today if you don't want to."

"I want to. Marie wants me to go. And the worst thing for me right now would be to stay here alone," Nico said. "Help me put the tent back up and arrange the camp, and we'll leave."

They had home-camp back in order in fifteen minutes, and downed a pot of coffee before going to the horses, at which point, Nico had to confess that he had never been on a horse and had no idea what to do. Pablito made no jokes or fuss, he just helped him get his foot into the stirrup and gave him a little boost up, then he took the time to adjust the length of both stirrups to fit him and cinched the saddle tight once more.

He told him how to give the horse a gentle tap with his heels to move and how to hold the reigns and pull to guide the horse, but the horse knew the way of the trail very well. He would follow Pablito's big gray with little need for input from Nico.

It was a two hour ride up a winding rocky trail to the high summer pasture, and Nico found the soft rolling and rocking of the horse almost hypnotic. He nearly fell asleep and came off the horse twice, but was awakened just in time by the creaking of the leather saddle as his body drifted to one side in slumber.

When they came over the last hill and into the pasture, the small herd was grazing exactly where Pablito said they would be. Fifteen horses of all colors the horse world has to offer; two young foals that both looked remarkably alike with a fuzzy light gray coat and black manes and tails; and one curious little slate colored burro that stayed out on the edge of the herd. He brayed with a laughing call as they came into view. The burros, as Pablito later told Nico, were always kept with the horses that free-grazed in the mountains because they were fearless at defending the herd from pumas.

Pablito had packed a lunch of dry sausage, hard cheese and fresh bread, and they spent some time at an old camp site on the edge of the pasture eating and sipping mate. Even this late in the season and on the verge of first snow fall, the high pasture was brilliant green Patagonian grasses, dotted with yellow dandelions and low growing vines that were covered in delicate white flowers shaped like tiny bells.

It was rimmed by tall basalt formations on the western side that shot straight up like a fortress wall, and shielded the horses from winds and rain coming in from the Pacific. When it did rain, it came down in a slow misty drizzle that saturated deeply into the top soil, and the grass roots were thick and strong as far down as a man would ever care to dig with a pick or shovel.

Pablito never had to worry about the horses wandering far from this summer pasture because there wasn't anything better to lure them away. The new foals always grew fat and strong here, and the only danger was an odd puma coming in to steal one of the young ones. Hence the burro.

The ride down with the herd was easy, as the horses all followed in line, aware that it was time to migrate to the warmer valley below. Nico wallowed lazily in the saddle in the warm sun and admired the view of the river and rolling green hills from above, but Pablito's mind was occupied by the thoughts of danger that could have killed his friend the night before.

Being on the edge of the wilderness alone, yet in easy reach of bad people from the roadway was a risky thing. He didn't realize until now that Nico had no way to defend himself. He knew Nico was lucky to survive that encounter, even if the thought hadn't occurred to Nico.

As his horse slowly clopped down the steep decline, planting one foot carefully before committing the next, he reached back to touch the handle of his constant companion, and the notion came to him. He decided that Nico needed a knife, and it was his duty as his only friend in this place to make sure he had a good one. A knife in this part of the world is not a tool so much as a companion that over time becomes a trusted friend. It will help you through the rigors of daily chores, and gracefully defend your life when trouble comes calling.

Pablito had many knives, and he treasured them all. They each had their place by his side at different times. His most useful blade was typical of the working gaucho, slender and long enough to penetrate deeply into the vital organs of a suffering cow, horse, or stag to end its misery, with a handle of aged oak wood.

It was made from carbon steel, not the fancy stainless steel that they sold in shops in the city to tourists and dudes. It had tarnished to a blue-black color over the decades from exposure to air and glinted a pearly rainbow patina when turned in the sunlight from the staining of blood and wine and oily hands. A true gaucho never scrubs his blade with soap and water, but wipes it clean with leather or wool and occasionally a little vino to cut the crusty residue. The edge will always be a brightly polished hint of the steel's true soul.

He also proudly wore his facón knife, inherited from his father, once a year during the parades and events at the *Puestero.* It was carried in a black leather sheath with silver trim on the tip, and had a shiny round handle carved from the blackest horn of some great animal he had never seen in person, but had been told they lived in some far off place in the world where giants and elephants still roamed. The facón was a killing blade.

PABLITO'S FATHER had taught him the elegant art of fighting with the knife in the way of South American street fighters (*el legado Andalùz*), a technique that originated in the knife fighting schools of southern Spain and traveled east with the immigrants to Central America. Pablito's father, Juan Carlos, was not a native Argentine nor even an originally raised gaucho.

He had grown up in the streets of a small city in Bolivia and was a street runner for the local Patron. He fled Bolivia when he tired of the constant danger of life in the city, and crossed the border into northern Argentina through the snake and mosquito infested jungles of Santa Fe Province. He heard wonderful tales of the gauchos who lived a free life in the open mountains and plains of Patagonia and made his way south, where he eventually found work on the French owned estancia.

Juan Carlos had learned the ways of tending horses and cows and eventually earned his own little puesto. His expertise with a blade came to bear as he began to carry the typical facón style knife favored by the gauchos, and his combat skills in *esgrima criollo*, as they called their knife fighting style, were legendary. The gauchos occasionally settled their differences with a quick blade, but those who lived and worked with Juan Carlos understood that a healthy respect ensured their survival.

It was a time honored tradition of passing down these skills from father to son, and even occasionally to a daughter. He taught Pablito to parry and thrust, and to deceive and distract and counterstrike with a slashing blade, and how to use his poncho wrapped around his free arm to fend off an attack.

Pablito never discussed it, but he had defended himself with the instincts honed by his father and a brutally sharp blade; on the day his father was murdered. Some people viewed it as rightful vengeance, and others as self defense, but it was the last time anyone looked at him as a small weak man. The reputation had followed him, and probably kept him from ever facing another argument. He was a calm, affable fellow, even shy; but he was also the kind of man not to be pushed into a corner.

* * *

PABLITO DELIVERED Nico back to his camp, then pushed the horses across the river to the winter valley alone. He returned to Nico's home-camp early the next morning.

He had thought about it for most of the night, and decided to trade him the trusty working knife that was passed to him after his brother died in a calf branding accident. It was medium length and served well for carving, eating or killing if necessary. He believed the knife and Nico would be worthy company for each other.

It had a properly aged steel backbone, hammered and forged in a furnace from the remnants of a large axle spring that had been liberated from a truck left unattended for too long in a deserted stretch of roadway. It was fitted with raw stag antler scales that over the years had worn down and now looked like finely polished ivory.

"Buen dia, Don Nico," he said as he rode into camp, just as Nico was lighting his morning fire.

"I enjoyed the ride yesterday, Pablito, but I can't do it again today. My ass is killing me," Nico said.

"No no, I have something I want to trade with you."

Pablito came down from his horse, and reached to the small of his back under his poncho and pulled out the stag handled knife in a handmade leather sheath with finely woven tips and trim. He gripped the handle and placed his thumb on the edge of the sheath, and in one motion pressed the sheath forward and withdrew the long blade. He reversed it deftly in his palm and offered it, handle first, to Nico.

"You need a knife, Don Nico, and this is a very fine one. It belonged to my brother, but he doesn't need it anymore," he said.

"Pablito, you bring me too many gifts. I can never repay them all," Nico said.

"This is not a gift," Pablito responded. "In Patagonia, we say a knife must never be given as a gift, or the blade will eventually cut the friendship. You must trade the knife for a coin."

"I have no coins to give you, Pablito. I have nothing."

"Then trade me with friendship. Nothing more. It's my knife, and I can ask whatever I want. That is what I want. But understand, to a gaucho friendship is no small thing," Pablito said. "Are you willing to trade me friendship?"

Nico looked at the diminutive gaucho, and again felt the emotion and surprise welling inside him. No one had ever surprised him so much in his life as this man, who possessed so little and gave so much with no prospect of future profit. Pablito valued another man's friendship above profit, as well as a simple life of working in the wild to garnering riches in the city.

It perplexed Nico. Actually, his own reaction to the gestures perplexed him more. He was moved to tears by something as lowly as honest friendship. He reached out and took the knife gently from the dark leathery hand of Pablito, and held it up in the morning sunlight to see the polished edge glinting back at him.

"I am. I'm willing," Nico said. "I'm beginning to understand what friendship is about."

A Companion

It was late April now, and the leaves were dark gold on the willows and the poplar trees that grew in small groves near the river and beginning to flutter to the ground with each new rise in the wind.

Nico made his way down to the river late this afternoon to cast sinking flies to the trout before the evening insect hatch started, because once it started the fish would only strike the floating surface flies, and he didn't have many more of those. Within 10 minutes he'd landed a nice rainbow trout and a beautifully spotted brown trout that were both perfect eating size. He took pleasure in using his new knife to clean them out on the shore and walked back to home-camp.

Darkness was setting in when he started a fire. He was leaning in and warming his hands over the flames while his fish were beginning to sizzle on the spit, when he caught the slightest movement in the corner of his eye from the bushes across the camp site. His hand eased around to the small of his back and found the stag handle of his knife. His fingers gripped it firmly, but he didn't draw it out just yet.

He was waiting see if he had really seen something or just imagined the movement, because the fire can make a man's eyes play tricks on him here in the dark desert night.

There it was a again. Something moved in the wind that he knew he'd never seen in that place before, and then it came forward. One slow step toward the camp fire, and just the face and neck became visible from the shadows. Its eyes reflected green from the flickering light as it stared directly into Nico's eyes, then it moved forward two more steps. It was a pitifully wretched looking dog.

His tangled, mud-soaked coat blended so well with the desert scrub that he was visible only to the keenest eye. His hair was matted with thorns and burs from the summer plants, and a single brilliant magenta flower from a milk thistle plant dangled from a dread-lock of fur on his neck. What looked like a hint of tiger stripes on his sides were actually his poorly covered ribs protruding beneath his skin. He was nearly starved to death.

Abandoned along the roadside months before by a family on vacation from the big city, he had no pride or fear left in him. His wild instincts to survive and hunt were coming to the surface, but the open plains of Patagonia were no place for a dog to be alone.

The constant hunger and loneliness left him stoic and mechanical in his pursuit of food. He scoured the roadside for tidbits and trash that might contain a crumb or morsel. He chased away the chimangos and vultures to grab a flattened greasy rabbit hide from the edge of the road, and devoured mice if he was lucky enough to catch one.

Sometimes a car would stop by the road to let a child out to pee, but if he dared come close they threw rocks at him, more often than a scrap of food. He wandered to the river's edge at night and drank deeply to fill his aching belly, then lay under the willow trees to sleep. As he grew weaker, the big gray desert foxes would come in late in the morning darkness to test his mettle and torment him.

He had smelled the fire from nearly a mile distant, and came to beg or steal a meal, and risk a beating at the hands of another cruel human. Nico looked across the firelight at the poor thing in the shadows that was looking back at him, and instantly saw his son Cristian's shining face.

"Can we keep him, Papa?" he said to Nico.

How many times he'd heard that over the years, and always he'd said, "No."

"He's starving Papa, and he doesn't have a home. He needs us," Cristian pleaded.

"We'll feed him this one time, and see what he does," Nico responded out loud.

He reached down and picked up the plastic bag with several ham and cheese sandwiches, that the bus driver had left in the little shrine along the roadside this morning. He pulled one out and tossed it across the fire to the ground in front of him.

At the tossing motion, and seeing something coming through the air in his direction, the dog wheeled and fled back to the safety of the brush because too many times before men threw stones or sticks to drive him away. He peeked slowly back into the firelight, and seeing the sandwich in the gravel, he lowered himself to the ground and crawled forward. He approached cautiously, and snatched the sandwich without ever taking his eyes off Nico. It was gone in a quick gulp without a single chew. Then he moved back one step and laid down facing Nico with a look of anticipation.

"I'll give you half my dinner tonight, dog, because my son wants me to feed you. But you be gone by morning," Nico said. Then he tossed the other sandwich, and this one didn't even hit the ground. The dog lurched up and caught it coming through the air, and again gulped it quickly and laid back down facing Nico. This time he raised and slowly wagged his matted tail from side to side, just twice.

Nico finished cooking his trout and sprinkled them with wild sage and a little of the mint that grows in great clumps along the shore line, and ate them while keeping an eye on his uninvited dinner guest.

The dog raised his head once when Nico pulled the first trout off the spit, but then put it back down and watched and dozed at the same time. He was exhausted, and this was the first thing he'd eaten in four days, since he came across the rotting remains of a rabbit killed by a car on the highway, and a truck nearly killed him too while he was trying to pry it from the tarmac.

Nico leaned back on Marie's bench and took a sip from the Irish whiskey bottle Jorge had left, and watched the sleepy dog in the flickering light. When the fire burned low he got up and headed to his tent and the warmth of his sleeping bag. The dog watched, but didn't move, and Nico turned before zipping up the tent flap and said, "Remember, this is just until morning."

He pulled himself into his feather filled bag and zipped it up around his chest the same as he'd done every night for many months now, but something felt different tonight. He could still hear Cristian's excited voice in his head, and tonight for the first time he didn't feel completely alone. He didn't care much for dogs before, he'd never had a dog. But just knowing that stray dog was laying outside his tent gave him a strange sense of comfort. It also made him feel like he just fulfilled a dream for his boy.

"If you're still here in the morning, I might have

some more food I can give you," he said through the tent wall.

The dog tiptoed close to the tent and curled up in a ball on top of the canvas duffle bag and buried his nose up under his tangled tail to keep it warm. Then he sighed with the contentment of food in his stomach, and to let Nico know that he was close.

Nico rose early the next morning and unzipped the tent door and stepped into the sunlight expecting, and secretly hoping, to see the dog still laying by his tent, but he was gone.

"Got his free meal and disappeared," he said.

"I figured."

But as he started a fresh fire to make some coffee and rattled a few cans looking through his food store, the dog bounded back into the clearing and sat across the fire pit with his tail sweeping a clean semi-circle in the sand. The small meal from the night before had revived him and he was up before sunrise following his instinct to hunt, but he wasn't going to wander far from the first man who had been kind to him in months, and he came running when he heard Nico moving around.

"You're still here?" he said, with a hint of happy surprise in his voice.

The dog cocked his ears forward and stood up on his feet and stared at Nico, as if something was about to happen.

"You're looking at me like I owe you money. Here's the last sandwich in my cache," he said. He reached into the bag and pulled out the remaining sandwich and held it out in his hand as he knelt down to the dog's level.

"You'll have to come take this one like a gentleman if you want anymore."

The dog approached slowly and cautiously with his head held in a respectfully bowed position but his eye cast upward, should a swinging hand come his way, but it didn't. He leaned up to the sandwich that Nico held lightly in the tips of his fingers, and with a reserve of confidence, he gently took the food in his teeth and pulled it away from the man's grasp. Then he lay down and ate it, still quickly, but not with the same panic of starvation as he'd eaten the night before.

Nico reached out and lightly ran the back of his knuckles, with his fingers rolled up to keep them safe from an unexpected snap, along the side of the dog's face and down his neck and back. When his hand approached the top of the dog's rump, the tips of his fingers and jagged overgrown nails lightly scratched that special place that brings a wave to the tail and unexpected pleasure. It was the first of many tedious steps to building trust.

Nico stuck to his normal routine that day. Coffee over the camp fire, then a long venture up river to fish and explore, followed by a watchful descent from the high hill down to the pullout to check the shrine for handouts. The dog was never more than two steps away from him during the entire day, except when he waded into the cold river to fish.

He started to wade in once after him, but changed his mind as the water was cold and fast, and he fled back to the rocky shore and whined and groaned until he realized Nico wasn't going to go any further. Then he found a nice sandy spot and lay down in the warm sun and dozed, but never so deeply that he wasn't aware of where Nico was at every second.

That night Nico sat on Marie's bench by the fire, silently watching the stars drifting overhead and the occasional streak of a flaming green rock falling from the depths of space to the earth. He waited patiently for her voice, but she was silent as well. He threw another large trunk on the fire as the cool autumn air chilled the camp, and the dog came cautiously around from the far side of the fire and curled up next to his feet by the bench.

They had shared a trout dinner together and split one of the sandwiches left in a bag in the shrine, and Nico was taking sips from a small bottle of Malbec that someone left as a special gift. Looking down at the shaggy mutt, he thought about the last time his son had fed the poor little dog outside the restaurant in Cruce del Desierto, and how deeply his heart ached when he saw a poor animal alone on the streets. Nico never understood until now.

He remembered hearing Cristian say, on more than one hopeful occasion, that if he ever got a dog of his very own he would call him Rocco. It was a fine strong name for a dog, and sounded as though it fit in nicely with his Italian heritage.

"Cristian wants to call you 'Rocco', what do you think of that?" he said to the dog.

The dog lay at his feet without any particular curiosity about the noises coming from the human, because in his experience when humans did make noises they didn't seem to indicate anything in particular, like a dog would bark with intention at a threatening intruder. Human sounds didn't seem to express any soulful emotion, like companionship or loneliness, like dogs often do when they close their eyes and turn their head to the night sky and howl for the world to know they are waiting for a friend.

So the human noises just seemed nonsensical to the dog, and he learned to ignore them. He paid more attention to the movements and expressions of the human animals. When they raised an arm, or quickly moved a leg, it was usually a threat. And he could readily determine from their facial features, because humans wear their intentions on their faces, if they were disposed to kindness or violence.

In the lines and shapes and furrows of Nico's face, the dog saw sadness. He sensed at any moment that Nico may turn his head to the stars and begin a chorus of sorrow.

Nico leaned over and made very direct eye contact with the dog, which tends to make dogs nervous because it feels aggressive, and he looked into his eyes and said, "Rocco. Your name is Rocco. Got it?"

Still nothing but a look of confusion from the dog; so this time he pulled a small bite of ham from the paper sandwich bag beside him, which immediately commanded attention from the dog.

With the dog's eyes now intently glued to the ham, Nico said, "Rocco!" The dog's ears perked and his head tilted slightly to the right, and Nico handed over the treat. Now he understood, the treats were called, "Rocco!"

For the next several weeks, Rocco paid close attention when this particular sound was made by the human, because it frequently meant that he was about to be fed. He later realized that it was in his interest to pay attention to the sound because it might mean that something else, either good or bad, was about to happen; this was obviously the human's alert sound. It might mean that food was being given away, or it might mean that the human wanted to stroke his coat and rub his belly, which he liked very much. It might also mean that danger was about, like one of those big loud vehicles on the highway was about to run him over. In any event he came to the conclusion that this particular sound should garner his immediate attention to his new human companion.

Rocco also became accustomed to Pablito's weekly passing by the home-camp and the glaring wary eyes from the big gray horse. He kept his distance, but also stayed within a protective space of Nico. He and Nico were a pack now, and he would defend him if he had to, and sensed Nico would defend him as well.

On one particular day, Nico and Rocco hiked very far up river to fish, walking along the exposed sandy shoreline and past the high cut-banks, and farther past the mouth of the Caleufu, which was down to just a trickle now this late in the season. Nico waded nearly to the opposite shoreline to fish the deepest channel, and Rocco took his normal vantage point on the shore to keep a watchful eye.

From the tree line on the opposite side of the river, Nico spotted Pablito coming down the path to the river, mounted on a new young horse, bay colored with a black-as-night mane and tail. The young horse was skittish as they came to the noisy river, and every little swaying branch and snapping twig made him dance and jerk his head. He was a working cattle horse in training. The new horse and his nervousness caught Rocco's eye, and he jumped to his feet at the ready.

Nico was close to the opposite shore and the water level was low, so he simple waded across and met Pablito in a grassy meadow on the other side. Rocco fell into an immediate panic. His human companion had never crossed the river before, and they had not been separated this far from each other for weeks. There was only one thing he could do. He had to swim across that river.

He paced up and down the shore and whined,

searching for an easy spot to cross but it all looked deep and fast and terrifying to a dog that had never spent any time in the water. He waded in slowly and retreated back to the shore twice, then at once he bolted straight into the current. He went jumping and splashing across, and everything seemed fine until he hit the deepest channel and all of a sudden he couldn't reach bottom any longer.

The river swept him downstream and dunked him twice under the rolling waves, but he came up paddling furiously and determined to reach the other side, and in just three more seconds he found the footing of the far bank beneath him, and relaxed as he came out and leaped up the steep face. He was freezing, soaked, and exhilarated at the same time.

Rocco came bounding from the river, flopped on his side and slid through the dry green grass and squirmed back and forth on his back, grunting like a little pig. He jumped to his feet and looked at Nico for the first time with something besides a look of hunger or fatigue in his eyes. He shook himself dry in a great spasm that started with a twisting of his head and his ears slapping from side to side, then his thin body snapped and sprayed water like a coiled spring wrapped in a wet cloth. It finished with a quivering matted tail.

For the first time in very long time, he felt the joy of reveling in the moment. He was thrilled to make it across the river, thrilled to be near his human, and just thrilled to be alive.

With a river-cleaned coat, Nico could see what Rocco really looked like underneath. He thought maybe a mix of german shepherd and terrier. He definitely had the look of a (Lady and the Tramp) union. The coarse hair and markings of a shepherd along his back and sides, with bristly hair around his face and legs. Not as big as a shepherd, not as small as a terrier. His left ear laid neatly folded forward like an airedale, and his right made a half-hearted effort to stand erect like a guard dog, but usually hung more out to the side rather than straight up. He gave the look of seriousness and comedy at the same time.

He had a sweetness and empathy in his eyes, and when Nico looked into them he knew that all this dog really wanted, was to belong. Then he saw something else. Something unexpected.

Nico wasn't an overly religious man, in fact he hadn't gone to church since he was young when his mother dragged him and his father to Christmas Mass. It wasn't a pleasant experience, nor unpleasant, he just didn't understand the fiery sermon and left with the feeling that he'd done something wrong, but no one would tell him exactly what it was. The notion of being guilty of some offense that he couldn't remember committing, made him uneasy about trusting in a deity he couldn't actually see or hear, or sit and chat things over with.

He wasn't an atheist either, he just didn't consider much about it one way or the other. God hadn't really played much of a role in his life as far as he could tell, nor in the lives of anyone around him. He watched people pray, including his own mother, for help and for health but never saw anything change in her life.

He knew people who used God's name in vulgar ways everyday of their lives, and they never seemed to pay any price for it. The only time in years he'd even spoken directly to God was when he screamed and cursed him in anger the day he stood in front of the little shrine after the trucker built it and lit the first candle. But it wasn't really God he was cursing that day. It was himself.

It seemed to Nico that Pablito had a strong spirituality, even though he rarely had the means to cart his family into a town where they could sit in a church and be told about God. It was more like he already had a very personal relationship with him. He saw the creator's hand in everything around him. The mountains, the river, the sky, and the animals and plants. He didn't need someone else to speak to God for him; he rode on horseback with God in his garden every day of his life.

But when Nico looked into Rocco's big almond colored eyes, he felt his heart ache like Cristian's had so many times, and wondered about a God that would allow so many poor helpless creatures to suffer and starve, or to die at the hands of men who lived without conscience for God's creations.

He also wondered why God would allow a foolish man like him to make mistakes that took the innocent lives of women and children, and live on. Maybe the living-on was his penance. To linger, and suffer in payment of the debt. Or maybe it was just God's way of giving him time to repent in his own way.

Nico was seeing the glint of a sorrowful God in the eyes of this pitiful dog. Even if he hadn't thought about God for years, maybe God was still thinking about him. He thought perhaps, in learning to love this poor creature, he was finding the path to his own redemption.

A Plan Of Revenge

In Buenos Aires, a war plan was being hatched and waged. Not in the streets, but in the offices of bankers and lawyers and speculators, and all of it being orchestrated from a shuttered study in a grand house in Recoleta.

Jacques d'Auvergne sat hunched over his mahogany desk in the shadows of his room, scheming to decimate the empire that Nico had built under his guidance. He helped him build it, and he could destroy it in just the same fashion. He would use every favor owed, every contact he could twist and leverage, and every dollar of his own fortune to make sure Nico's businesses collapsed and left him penniless if he ever dared to return to the city. He would be living in the streets and begging for meals when he came back.

But it wouldn't be accomplished without risk. Jacques first thought to push the bankers he introduced to Nico years ago to close off his lines of credit and call the notes due on the companies, which he assumed would force them into bankruptcy. But Nico had been smart. As the two big companies prospered, he had ignored Jacques' advice to continue borrowing the bankers' money and expand, and instead heeded his real father's advice.

He payed off the debt, and bought land and assets. The building that his father rented and all of the special tooling was the first thing he bought, guaranteeing his father would always have his own shop. Then he bought the timberland in Patagonia that bordered the Caleufu River to the south of San Martin de Los Andes. This he did at Marie's suggestion. She knew the raw materials were the biggest expense in the business, and the land could be purchased at that time for a fraction of its future value; and she dreamed of living in those very mountains one day.

The workers in the companies were organized, and Nico was seen as a generous contributor when the influence of politics or business made their lives difficult. His businesses were among those who never had problems with the big union bosses of the province, and he protected the workers. He came from the same streets as most of them, and they looked at him as a hero of the common man. He might have lived in a big house, driven a German car and fished with the President, but he treated his employees like family.

They never went hungry, nor did their children want

for a gift under the tree at Christmas, nor was a day of rest not given when sorely needed. When Nico's bitter father-in-law tried to leverage his commercial contacts to pressure suppliers and delivery truck drivers and distributors and longshoremen to cripple Nico's supply chain, he was met with a wall of violent resistance.

Jacques' only play became the most dangerous one he could make. He had to turn his own investments into cash, form a larger investment group with his financial allies, and risk it by purchasing a company to compete against Azzarà Industries. Then he paid huge bribes to steal away their contracts.

It was an enormous gamble with his family's fortune. He would have to successfully run those companies and drive Nico's to dust, or return to the dust himself. What Jacques didn't realize, is that Nico was not the one he was waging war against. It was Jorge Rodriguez.

Jorge had friends in high places, and when the news reached his ears he was quick to understand Jacques' intentions and stayed two steps ahead of him from that moment. When it was apparent that Nico would not be soon returning from the high river bank along the Limay, Jorge started quickly moving pieces on the chess board.

He had seeded the company board of directors with close friends and lawyers with common business interests, and after thirty days of absence, he had Nico declared incompetent to continue as Chairman. He was voted into the role and given complete autonomy. In the months that followed, he began laying the groundwork to carve up and sell the companies for a significant profit.

Jacques set his sights on the largest furniture maker in all of South America, Saragon Manufacturing Corporation, and after months of negotiating he paid an enormous sum for a behemoth of a company. But Jorge had laid a clever trap.

While Jacques was trying to leverage the purchase of Saragon, Jorge was selling all of the assets of Nico's companies *to* Saragon through a secret holding company in Barbados. Instead of buying a dominant competitor to Nico's company, Jacques' investment group ended up paying an inflated price for a company that was deep in debt. It was a financial disaster of epic proportions.

While other chaos from the communists and the anti-communists kept the newspapers churning, and spread fear among the citizens of Buenos Aires, the old guard of the city behind the scenes were skittering around like so many little cockroaches that just received a foot stomping. The men who sat in lavish offices smoking cigars and plotting profits to add to their great fortunes had felt the sting of their own lash, and many bank accounts had been diminished.

The financial failure wounded many of the men who had never worked a real job in their lives, but none worse than the man who orchestrated the whole affair, Jacques. In seeking revenge against his son-in-law, he had only managed to squander his family's fortune, amassed over several generations, and he was left with nothing more than the house he lived in, and a small monthly stipend from a trust fund that he wasn't able to raid in the effort.

Jorge, on the other hand, came out smelling like a freshly trimmed rose. He took the majority of Azzarà Industries' assets while they were under his personal hand, and sold them through the back door for twenty percent more than they were worth, to the same pirate who was trying to set fire to them from the front door.

He was now sitting on a mountain of cash. He formed a new corporation, Southern Cross Ventures, and began the next phase of his grand plan. The plan he'd been hatching for months now, since the day Nico smashed the bones in his arm.

The Snows of Winter

❧

A thundering rumble broke the silence and startled Nico from a deep sleep, but he was still enveloped in darkness and he felt bound and tied in the sleeping bag. He thrashed and flailed inside the mummy wrapping in a panic until he came to his senses and found the internal zipper and jerked it down to his feet and sprung himself free.

Out of instinct and lingering paranoia, he reached for the knife that he now kept tucked inside the rolled blanket that he slept with under his head. His first thought was that someone was coming for him. Perhaps the robbers had returned for vengeance, or maybe the men in the black car were sneaking in under the cover of darkness. Outside the tent, Rocco was growling and huffing threatening muffled barks at whatever unknown sound had brought him to full alert.

There was a secondary, low thudding sound, high

above them on the mountain, and a series of clanging, banging and metallic screeching, followed by the clear sound of gravel and rock tumbling. It sounded like another car had just flung itself from the roadway and was tumbling down the hillside.

In seconds, the echoes of the unknown catastrophe faded and the night was silent again, save for the faint sound of a big diesel-engined truck slowly navigating its way up the highway. Nico crawled outside the tent into a clear night sky, but he couldn't see anything or hear anything more, and he wondered if some other poor soul was trapped in a crushed vehicle on the hill.

Rocco came to his side and stood leaning lightly against him, and they both felt a little comforting reassurance in the contact, as they scanned into the darkness for any signs of movement or sounds, but there was nothing. All he could do was wait until sunrise in another hour.

He started off, with Rocco leading, as soon as he could clearly see the outlines of rocks and shrubs, and they were well on the way up the hill when the sun finally crested. The climb was difficult, and it took him nearly thirty minutes to cover only two hundred yards up the face before he came upon the source of the early morning noise.

To his relief, it wasn't a car full of people. There were no bodies or gruesome discoveries, but something more intriguing. A pile of building materials had broken free from a delivery truck and tumbled over the ledge and collected into a pile against the same rocky ledge that broke Nico's fall that fateful day.

During an early run up the mountain road in total darkness, the driver had over-corrected on the sharp corner and caused a poorly tied rope to break free and dumped half of the cargo bound for a home building delivery, over the side. He couldn't stop on the steep hill or he would never have been able to get started again, so he kept on going up the road at full power in low gear. It wasn't the first time cargo was lost from an open flatbed trailer on this twisting highway, and certainly wouldn't be the last.

It was a fortunate accident for Nico, because there were enough full sections of plywood and tin roofing to piece together a small shed that would keep the rain and wind, and very soon the snow, at bay. It wouldn't be anything fancy, but at least something more comfortable and roomy than the small tent he was living in now, and certainly warmer in the winter.

Constructing the small cabin would be the easy part though. The real challenge at hand was getting the materials down the treacherous hillside. The plywood was bulky and heavy. Each piece had to be pulled down the slope by holding the leading edge behind him or above his head, and inching his way down.

He stopped to rest every five or ten minutes to catch his breath and let his shoulders recover from the awkward position, but the balancing of the load going down a steep slope of loose rock and gravel was putting tremendous strain on his back and his knees. Every time a slight gust of wind arose and caught hold of the plywood like a wooden sail, it would wrench his body sideways or threaten to send him tumbling down the mountain in a heap. It took him four hours and five trips back up to the pile just to bring all of the wood down.

Three long sheets of tin roofing material were scattered along the outcropping. He gathered those and stacked them on top of each other, and he also found a large roll of thin tie wire, and lashed that to the top of the pile. The tin sheets were extruded into a rounded wave pattern, and they nested together easily and slid down the slope with little effort, but he had to control the pace or they willingly broke away from his grasp and went flying out of control. These roof sections were like a gift from heaven, and he didn't want them damaged on the way down the hill.

By mid-afternoon he had finished the transport to home-camp of everything from the fallen cargo treasure. He was completely exhausted and his back and legs were strained and aching, so much so that he didn't have the energy or the enthusiasm to even walk to the river and make a few casts to raise a trout for dinner. He was so tired that his hunger retreated in lieu of his need for sleep, and he crawled into his tent and pulled the warm duck down bag around him and drifted off.

Rocco was tired as well from following up and down all day and carefully inspecting and marking their new property, and he curled up on the canvas bag next to the tent that had become his own bed, and fell asleep. But his empty stomach gurgled and groaned throughout the night.

The next morning, Nico surveyed his haul. He had five sections of three-quarter inch plywood, three sections of roofing tin, one roll of light flexible wire and he found the thirty foot long length of rope that snapped and discharged the materials, up on the edge of the highway. He still had a dozen long poles of quebracho wood left from the panicked trucker's mad escape, and they would make for very strong corner posts and roof supports.

Before beginning his new construction project, he made hot coffee over the fire pit, and threw two large trunks of wood on the fire to burn down while he walked to the river and caught breakfast. He didn't think it would take long, and the coals should be glowing well for cooking by the time he came back.

The river was at its seasonal low now, with the final snow at the tops of the mountains having fully melted away last month, and the autumn rains and snow due to start soon. Nico was able to walk across the gravel bars that were fully exposed, so he could stand and cast to the furthest part of the opposite shore, to the cut-bank under the willow trees, which were now stripped completely bare of leaves by the gorging larvae of summer wasps. The branches looked like long, thick strands of hair flowing up and down in the breeze.

He sensed there was something different in the river today. The small fish and minnows that normally hover close to the bank and rarely move to deeper water, were restless, and he could see them breaking from cover and racing back and forth across the main current. He wondered if the demon fish was still there under the cut-bank, and moving to hunt during the daylight hours now. Maybe he wasn't getting his fill of hapless creatures that crossed the river at night, and he was hungry enough now to chase the small fry to fill his belly.

Nico lowered himself to the gravel to minimize his profile, and slowly crawled on his hands and knees closer to the narrow river channel, thinking there might be a chance to look the demon directly in the eye. He inched up closer and peered into the crystalline water, searching for his nemesis.

"Where are you, you evil monster?" he whispered. Then he squinted into the sun sparkled reflections in the river.

He saw a long dark shadow rippling across the rocky bottom and moving upstream, but the fish was so well camouflaged he never saw him, just his shadow.

"There you are! You've given yourself away demon."

Then, another massive shadow came gliding past him, and a third as big or bigger than the first. It seemed he had stirred up an entire nest of river demons! A hundred yards upstream there was an explosion on the surface, at a place in the river where a rocky ledge was now exposed by the low water and it formed a wide cascade of bubbling foam as the river poured over the ledge and into the next level below. Small fish were racing and flying through the air, and a dozen or more huge trout were slashing them to pieces, leaping out of the water to catch them in mid-air. It was a massacre.

Today was the day of the deadly run. The day when millions of newly hatched minnows make one collective and desperate run down the river to reach the deep lake where they will spend the rest of their lives, if they make it through the gauntlet. The old cannibalistic trout were waiting for them. They waited all year for this one day to gorge on the young of others.

Nico quickly cut off the foam bug fly he had on his line, and tied on another that was white and silver, with large black beads on the front that looked like terrified eyes. He hoped it would be a close enough resemblance to the minnows to fool a huge rainbow trout.

He leapt to his feet and made a dash for the cascading water, stripping out line from the reel with his left hand as he ran to make a quick cast. He was already gaining momentum with two false casts before he stopped running, and as he planted his foot the fly was sailing on its way.

The white and silver fly landed above the cascading drop-off, just where he intended, and he stripped the line in quickly to move the fly as if it were a tiny fish swimming in a panic. It worked. As the little fly hit the lower pool of water, it was engulfed by a twenty five inch long rainbow trout leaping upward with a gaping mouth.

Nico instantly pulled the line tight, and raised his rod to set the hook. The fish broke away from the cascade, and raced downstream with the strong current propelling him even faster, and Nico had to run down the river bank after him to keep the giant fish from breaking his rod.

The fish would double back upstream for a short burst, then turn again into the deep current that was flowing to its final destination in the Atlantic. Nico kept pace, leaping and stumbling through brush and thorn on the river's edge with Rocco bounding behind and barking a song of encouragement. But the giant had the edge in this fast water, and the feeble, cheap fly rod creaked and groaned under his weight. With every violent snap and jerk, Nico feared the rod was about to break.

"I can't lose this rod, it's all I have!" he thought to himself. "I can't catch this fish, he's too big. He's going to break my rod, then I'll have nothing."

Then he heard Cristian's voice in his ear.

"You've got him Papa! Hold on to him, hold on to him!" he yelled.

And Nico held on.

The battle ended over a hundred yards farther downstream, as the fish reached a deep pool of slow moving water, and with no strong current to use for his advantage it was only minutes before he rolled to his side and accepted his fate into Nico's outstretched hand. Cristian was there with him when the giant came to hand, exhausted and defeated, and Nico could see him gripping the fish by its mighty tail with both his small hands and lifting him from the water.

Nico smiled at his son, and felt his heart swell ever so slightly. He held that vision in his mind for most of the day, pausing occasionally to recall the battle, and always seeing Cristian in the middle of the fray along side him.

He hated to kill the big fish, but it was large enough to feed both Nico and Rocco for the whole day. "You fought a brave fight and I'm sorry to kill you my friend, but this is what I do," he said.

He ended it quickly, and cleaned the fish in the clear water. Then hung it on a green willow branch to sizzle over the coals while he started the construction of his winter cabin.

HE PLANTED the four corner posts deeply into the ground and pounded rocks in around them until they were straight and solid. He carved joints to connect the beams around the top, and hoisted the remaining posts above and set them at a steep angle downward to the west, with the opening to the eastern horizon.

The wind and snow blew consistently from the west, so his meager doorway, made from the tattered tent stretched across a frame, would face away from the blow. The wood panels were all smartly attached and joined at angles that wouldn't allow the rain to blow through, and the tin sheets were placed on the roof beams and overlapped so melting snow would run off to the west and downhill away from the shack.

All of the junctures and joints he bound tightly with the thin rusting wire, and to keep the roof held firmly down in place when the wind blew strong, he pulled the four wheels and tires from the wreck and placed them on top, as he had seen so many times on the shanties and shacks of campesinos who lived near the highway.

It was wide enough for him to lay completely stretched out, and tall enough to stand fully erect, about the same dimensions perhaps as an average prison cell, but his first nights in the new home made him feel almost guilty for allowing himself the new level of luxury. His first days laying in the back of the wreck, and the following months laying on the cold hard ground in the sleeping bag in the tent, had felt oddly like a punishment that he deserved.

The sun was a veiled glowing ball that traveled above the dense cloud cover now, nearly every day for the past week. Its path had changed dramatically with the season. Where it once careened straight overhead from Buenos Aires and landed due west over San Martin de Los Andes, it was now gliding in a shallow arc that barely rose above the hills to the north before falling short of the Lanin volcano.

The steady cloud drift was drizzling rain off and on until the air from Antarctica came crawling up the coast. Then snow fell like freshly plucked goose down, flittering from the sky. Just a few flakes here and there at first, then it came in earnest, making it difficult to see even as far as the river from home-camp through the windblown snow.

Nico didn't stop to consider his fortune in having the makings of a solid structure fall in his lap so soon before. Being wet and freezing with no place to store and dry a regular supply of wood could have been a deadly turn of events for him. Mother Nature feels no pity or remorse for the weak or wounded, nor for the broken-hearted. There were barely eight hours of daylight now, which limited his time to fish, cook, and gather wood for the days ahead. His exploration of the surrounding hills and mountains would be limited to rare days of the hot *zonda winds*, when they blew down from the north.

He used a wrench from the tool kit in the trunk of the car to take out the screws and pull out the leather rear seat, and he moved it into his little make-shift cabin to serve as a bed above the cold ground. It was more comfortable, but more than that, he liked the smell of the leather. It rekindled pleasant memories of Cristian, stretched peacefully over the seat on long drives across country. The open space in the back of the car became his storage for firewood, and he kept sections of dried limbs and branches that he gathered along the shoreline stacked neatly out of the rain.

The last thing he did was to take Marie and Cristian's luggage bags from the trunk and bring them into the shelter. He put Cristian's in the front corner, and placed his little backpack with his clothes safely on top. Marie's bag, he placed next to the head of his bed.

He built a true winter fire that night to warm the camp, and was sitting out late, finishing the bits of his latest catch and tossing a few fatty pieces to Rocco when the snow started falling again. He turned his eyes up to the darkness and watched the flakes appearing from the black and drifting down to land on his cheeks and nose, and blanketing everything around him in a slow building dust that glowed red from the firelight.

The night sounds of the desert and mountains always ceased into a perfectly muted silence when the snows came, as if all living things were huddled safely somewhere and all of the normal activities of life paused to watch the snow falling. Everything except the river, which still rolled and gurgled through the night.

Nico shook the snow from his poncho and his hair and went into the shack, and he stretched the sleeping bag over the leather seat, sat on the edge, and pulled off the rubber boots that Jorge had left him and placed them side by side underneath. It felt like the most civilized thing he had done in a long time.

Light flickered inside from the remains of the fire glowing through the tent-door, then suddenly beneath it came a shiny wet nose. Not the whole head, just the nose, followed by a long slow inhale, and a heavy soulful sigh. He couldn't help but smile, and he didn't scold him because he knew it was snowing heavily outside now. He didn't blame him for making a subtle plea to come inside and out of the cold.

"Can't handle a little snow?" he said to the nose.

The nose didn't move, but he could see the shadow of a tail slowly waving in the firelight through the thin fabric door.

"Get in here, Roc..."

Before he finished saying his name, Rocco shot through the crack in the door, and not daring to push his luck too far, he curled instantly into a ball to the side of the opening next to Cristian's suitcase, as if he knew where he belonged. He groaned another sigh of bliss, and covered his face with his tail and closed his eyes. "So you're a house dog now?" Nico said. Then he laughed, and fell over on the leather bed and pulled the warm down bag up around him and slept deeply and peacefully as winter covered the world around them.

The Day of the Lupins

Nico came out of his little shack and stood facing east in the morning sun, like he always did, although it wasn't always sunny. Sometimes the rain was blistering on the tin roof of the shack, or the wind was trying to rip it completely off. During the cold desert winter he woke up to fresh snow on the ground, but it usually melted by late morning. But today the sun was shining and the air was crisp and out of nowhere, the first lupin flowers were starting to bloom along the river in an array of blues and purples and pinks. Spring had finally come.

Nico and Rocco had huddled through the winter, braving the cold days and colder nights. Pablito may have saved their lives by bringing in an old oil drum that had been cut and fitted with an exhaust pipe and used as a campesino wood stove. They brought into the shack and plumbed the exhaust up through the roof. It made for more comfortable sleeping at night, and Nico frequently woke in the morning to find Rocco curled up in front of the stove as it cooled.

He still built camp fires to sit out sometimes and chat with Marie at night when the stars were full, but not as often.

The fishing was not as good during the winter months because the trout were chilled and sluggish themselves. They didn't feed as intensely during the winter, and there were fewer insect hatches and creatures in the river during winter to keep them in an active frenzy. So, Nico caught what he could, and relied on the regular generosity of the bus drivers and their steady diet of ham sandwiches and sometimes a small sample bottle of wine. Pablito's early morning visits with fresh bread and marmalade were eagerly awaited too, and throughout the long winter he never failed to come by at least once a week to check on them and share a meal and some mate or coffee.

Along with the lupins blooming on this warm spring day came the first flashes of rising water in the river as the snow in the mountains began to thaw and run to the ocean. The new water came in bursts, and was muddy at first, ripping soil and dirt from the dry trails up river, then later changed to silty gray from the old snow before running crystal clear. Nico couldn't fish during those few days, but it passed quickly, and in the meantime he and Rocco ventured up river again on long daily hikes and climbs.

On the first big bend of the river west of home-camp, the opposite shoreline was a tall bank, over fifty feet high, of ancient sandstone that was never flooded. It was peppered with holes, dug out by the desert parrots that nested in the rock face every year, and looked like an enormous apartment complex you might see in any big city.

The early parrots were just starting to take up residence, and they peered out as Nico and Rocco walked by. They were green and gold and blue, with long tail feathers of flaming red that trailed behind, and they babbled and chattered and squawked at the intruders. It would soon be a colony of thousands living in the burrows and raising their young until late summer, then they would migrate back into the desert to forage in one grand flock.

As they came back by the river to home-camp, Nico paused to look across at the line of willows along the opposite shore and the new green leaf buds just starting to pop into view, and he wondered about the demon fish that lived in the deep channel beneath them. He hadn't seen or heard him during the long winter, but he knew he was still there, waiting for the river to fill with fresh living things again.

As he stood there staring into the water, searching for a sign of the demon, he heard the familiar clatter of hooves coming along the rocky trail, and he smiled as he turned, knowing it was Pablito.

"Hola, Pablito," he said. "Is it almost time to take the horses back up to the summer pasture?"

"In a few weeks more, but we have something more important to tend to," Pablito said. "We have a tradition here in the spring. Every year when the lupins bloom, we make an asado outside in the garden, and my family wants you to come join us this year. It will be day after tomorrow, because I have to find a nice young goat to roast, but I will come early in the morning with a horse for you."

"Pablito, I'm not sure I can make it," Nico responded. He tilted his head down and kicked lightly at the gravel under his feet.

"Why?"

"Because I just can't," Nico said. Now there was a nervous irritation in his voice.

Pablito climbed down from the big gray and walked deliberately to Nico, stopping inches away from him and stared upward into his eyes. "Why won't you come to have asado with my family? Is my family not good enough for you?"

"That doesn't have anything to do with it. I never said that," Nico answered. Then he pivoted away from Pablito and turned to walk up to camp, but Pablito ran around him and cut him off, standing firmly in front of him again.

"I've been telling my family about you for over a year. I've told them about my friend, Nico. And they want to meet you. Now tell me the truth. Why won't you come to meet my family?"

"Because the last time I was in the company of a woman and child, they died! They died, Pablito!" he said with quivering anger. Then he visibly shrank, and his shoulders fell to the sides and his head hung limply, staring at the ground.

Pablito grabbed him by the arms and shook his face upright, and when he held his gaze he spoke in a calm voice. "Nico, I've talked with the police and the Gendarmerie who investigated that accident. And that's all it was. An accident. You had no way of knowing that gravel was washed across the road that day. People die in accidents every day. My brother died in an accident. We've all lost people, Nico. It isn't always someone's fault."

Then Pablito followed more firmly, "Now tell me Nico, are you my friend?"

"Yes. I am your friend, and you are the only friend I have in the world," Nico said.

"Then I want to introduce my friend to my family, and have a meal together like friends do."

Nico took a deep breath, let it out slowly, and nodded his head.

Two days later, Nico walked down to the river where a shallow calm pool formed to the side from the rising spring water, and stooped over to fill his pot to make some coffee. The water was flat and reflective like a mirror, and he looked at his scruffy beard and tangled hair and thought, "I better do something about this, or I'll frighten Pablito's children if I show up looking like a wild creature from the forest!" So he pulled off his dirty clothes and jumped straight into the freezing water before he lost his nerve, and it was like a jolt of lightning striking his body.

"Ahhh!" he screamed, as he came up for air, but the numbness set in quickly and he dunked his head and scrubbed the filth from his hair and his beard. Then he let the fresh running river wash the soil and stink from his body. Rocco thought it was a grand game, and came bounding into the water with him, but quickly changed his mind and jumped back to the bank, and shook himself madly to dry his coat.

"Get yourself clean, Rocco. We don't want to offend our hosts," he said. Rocco shook his thick coat out again and shivered with a great tremor that started at his nose and rolled through his body to the tip of his tail.

When he felt clean enough and his fingers turned a light shade of purple, Nico came clambering out of the river and the cool morning air shocked his skin to the texture of a freshly plucked hen. He ran to the morning fire and huddled over it for a few minutes to get the blood flowing again, before he pulled out a mostly clean pair of trousers that he had stored in his suitcase, and a clean shirt that was still neatly folded and pressed from the year before. He pulled out his shaving kit, ignored and unused for a very long time, and took a small pair of scissors and trimmed his beard and cut out some of the knots and tangles from his hair and combed it back. At least now he would look more presentable to meet Pablito's family.

He was feeling anxious in a way he hadn't for a long time. Being with other people, having conversation, sharing a meal; it frightened him. Pablito and Rocco had been his only (living) company for a very long time.

He could hear Pablito coming along the stone path shortly after, with a second horse in tow for him. He smiled with surprise when he saw Nico with clean clothes and his beard and hair trimmed.

"Hola, Nico. Are you ready?" he said.

"Yes, and I bathed!"

Nico went in to the shack to fetch his poncho for the early morning ride into the mountains, then he pulled himself up and settled his feet into the stirrups, and gently tapped the horse in the sides with his heel. They moved down the well-worn trail above the driftwood and along the river bank, with Rocco bounding along behind, for three miles until reaching the wide vado. Then they urged the horses across the shallow water to the southern side of the river and headed up into the forested hillside.

As they reached the upper tree line, Nico pulled back lightly on the reigns and pivoted his horse to take a look down over the river and the three rows of hills that obscured his view of home-camp. This was the farthest he had been away from Marie and Cristian since the day of the accident.

In his heart he knew that going one step more would be the beginning of a completely different life for him. He could feel it. Something about the world around him was changing. He was reaching a threshold that had to be crossed.

Pablito turned and asked, "Is everything alright, Nico?"

"Yes. I just needed to see what lay behind me," Nico said.

They pulled up the trail and slowly climbed through a forest of elegant Coihue trees and farther up into a small grove of the prehistoric looking Araucarias, that the British called "monkey puzzle trees". They tower over two hundred feet tall and are covered with spiny scales that looked reptilian. The trail went over a hill, and down into a sheltered valley that was lined with poplars and columned cypress trees, then into an open green pasture.

On the edge of the south side of the pasture, framed by the pine forest behind, was a white stone cottage house with a clay colored roof and a tiled gallery wrapped around the western side. It resembled the Andalusian style homes in the horse country outside of Buenos Aires that Marie loved so much.

The horses came to a sudden halt in the center of the pasture, lured by the lush green grasses of primavera and yellow dandelions, and they paused and dropped the reins to let them have their fill.

"Does anyone live in that house, Pablito?" Nico asked.

"No. It has never been lived in. The owner of the estancia built it many years ago for his daughter, who lived far away from here, but she never came." he said. "My wife comes and keeps it clean inside, but the outside needs some work now, and the owner doesn't care about it so he won't pay to keep it up. It's a shame no one lives in it, it's a very beautiful house."

They pulled the horses' heads up from the grass and continued just along a trail through the next stand of trees, to arrive at Pablito's cabin. It sat in a clearing with tall grass and fruit trees that were so old they no longer produced fruit, but they were beautifully ancient, and the children loved to climb them and the birds roosted and nested every year in their branches.

They would have made good firewood for many winters, but Pablito thought they brought so much joy to the home that it was better to let them live out their days in peace as part of the family. They had grown here through the generations of the original French homesteaders. They fed them and their children with fresh fruit, and then Pablito's parents; and he had memories of playing in their branches and boughs himself as a boy. It would have been like killing a member of the family to chop them down.

Pablito's two daughters came running out to greet

them as they tied the horses to a rail fence, and they were thrilled to finally meet Nico, as they had been hearing stories about him from their father for the past year. They also heard stories about him on occasion from the other children in the local school that they attended three days a week, and those stories painted a very different picture, so they were curious to see which stories were true.

Wearing matching flowered summer dresses, with their dark straight hair pulled back into long braided ponytails with a ribbon at the end, one pink and the other green, they stood side by side, and waited patiently for their father to introduce them. First one, and then the other, and as their name was called they stepped forward and leaned up on their tiptoes to offer their right cheek for a formal greeting kiss and said, "Encantada, Señor Azzará."

He didn't look anything like what they expected. The other children told tales of a hideous monster, deformed and scarred by the terrible car crashing down the mountainside, and they said he lived in a cave by the river and attacked anyone who came near. They said he ate small animals and fish raw with his hands, and would even devour a child if he could catch one.

Pablito's daughters didn't believe all of these things because their father told them different, but still, they were not expecting to see a man who looked so normal, and kind. One leaned over and whispered something into the ear of the other, and they both erupted into giggles.

"What's so funny?" Nico asked.

"You're very handsome for a monster!" said the youngest. Then they both laughed, and turned and ran away.

Nico smiled, and Pablito turned red, but just shrugged his shoulders, with an apologetic grin.

Pablito's wife, Juanita, came from inside the cabin wearing a blue blouse and a long, dark red skirt, along with a smile like morning sunshine. She embraced Nico and kissed his cheek as if he were a member of their family who had been away for a long time.

"Welcome Nicholas," she said, as if she had known him all his life.

"Thank you for inviting me to your home, Juanita," Nico replied.

Her warmth, and the way it made him feel to be held in such an innocent embrace took him by surprise. He'd forgotten so many things about the world that circulated around him, while he sat for so long in one lonely place.

This was the first woman in over a year to put her arms around him. The first woman he had even seen in over a year. He spent most of last night in fear of the sight of her. And here she was, warming his heart in an instant.

Rocco was even greeted by Pablito's two dogs with wagging tails and curious noses, and they sniffed and investigated him thoroughly before they all three went bounding off into the trees behind the cabin with the girls.

An open asado pit was glowing with a fire that Pablito started before he left early in the morning to fetch Nico, and a chivo was slowly roasting on a rack in front of the coals. A small grill on the side had other small cuts of meat and vegetables wrapped in tin and simmering.

They sat on a long wooden bench on the outside edge of the pit under the tree canopy, and Juanita came with glasses and a cold bottle of Quilmes beer for the men, as they had just traveled a long distance on horseback and looked quite thirsty. They clinked their glasses and said, "Salud", then took long deep drinks of the soothing cold beer.

An asado isn't so much a meal as it is a grand social event. Even with only a handful of people, it's about rituals of preparation and cooking, and old, time honored traditions. The men have roles and the women have theirs. There was a long table made from pine wood planks with green colored marbling, and a setting for everyone with a round carved wood plate, a knife and fork, a plastic cup for water and a store bought glass for wine for the adults.

As the time grew near to sit and eat together, Juanita brought side dishes and drinks to the table, and a large bowl filled with fresh bread, covered with a white kitchen towel to keep it warm. She placed a thick golden biscuit directly on the table in front of each place setting, and poured fresh cool water into everyone's cup, and as Nico came to sit at his place, she opened a bottle of Bonarda table wine and filled his glass.

"Thank you. It has been a long time since a beautiful woman filled my glass at the table," he said, as his mind drifted back to an image of Marie.

She and the girls took their places at the table, and Pablito came with a large tray covered with a selection of cuts from the chorizo sausages, serving Juanita first and then his daughters, and finally Nico and himself last. Later he came again to serve everyone with the main course of chivo, and continued making his way back and forth to everyone at the table until they begged him to stop.

It was an elegant meal made from the most simple of foods, served in a beautifully natural setting, and decorated with conversation and the laughter of little girls. Nico was absorbed in the scene around him, and thought about his own life at the same time, and oddly, how much he found himself in envy of this little gaucho.

Pablito lived in a tiny cabin provided by the land owner, and he worked hard every day for a meager wage. He owned very little. Two changes of clothes, a few knives and tools, and three horses were the extent of his worldly possessions. But surrounding him was a loving family, a wife and two beautiful, happy children.

He lived in a peaceful place, and enjoyed his life. He

was the man he was supposed to be, and he wanted nothing more. He lived with joy in his heart. He had none of what Nico once had; and yet, everything he did not.

When Nico was young he resented having so little, and it drove him to seek riches. If he were rich he thought he could buy everything he needed to make himself and his family happy. But here he sat, among a small family happier than any he had ever known, and they were not rich. Then it came to him.

Real wealth is measured in joy. The person who finds the most joy in living has surely lived the most; and it waits all around us to be found. It waits in the cool green waters and the calling to the fly. It waits in the laughter of a child, in the sparkling eye of a dog, and on the crest of a mountain above the clouds. It waits in the warming thump of a woman's heartbeat with your ear lain softly across her smooth belly.

Joy waits to be sought and found in the deepest recesses of your soul. It lays silently in each of us waiting to be discovered by the rolling over of a stone, or opening of a long-locked chest. But it can't be plucked from a shelf and bought. Joy is a living thing that is seeded and grows, and spreads to other fields as the windblown weed.

The seeds of joy are akin to the seeds of the wild grasses and flowers that lay buried everywhere in the soil, waiting for just a drop of rain and a ray of sun to animate them into the living, and there is a color of joy for any occasion. The most barren, blown and scorched desert that appears as an utterly dead place, becomes a canvas of color and flowers with a single light drizzle.

This is the truth of the human experience, that any joy bought can be taken away, or will soon enough break or wear into uselessness. But natural joy, seeded and grown will replenish itself over and again.

Many hours passed before Juanita and the girls started clearing the table, and Pablito asked Nico if he would like to open another bottle of wine, but he was in the mood for a nice long walk.

"On the other side of the house is a trail that follows the stream up the mountain, and there is a beautiful view from the ridge. You would enjoy it," Pablito said.

So he followed the trail up, and Rocco came bounding behind him, never to be far from his sight. The trail went through an old apple grove and into a thicket of tall birch trees with silvery bark that peeled as they aged, and the ground beneath them was covered two feet deep with the fallen leaves from last year. Then he passed a break in the trees, and it turned into a forest of ancient Oregon pines, long past their time to harvest, that continued straight up the vertical slope.

Beneath the pines was a ground cover of vining plants with waxy green leaves and pale blue flowers, and in shaded places where the stream ran alongside the trail he saw wild orchids with white and purple stripes and crimson eyes. The last two hundred yards of the trail, he flushed coveys of quail, forty or fifty at a time, with celeste blue breasts and a teardrop feather hanging forward over their little heads. They kept flushing, and flushing until he reached the top of the ridge and he realized it had been one great covey of birds that numbered over three hundred strong.

At the top of the ridge he turned and looked back to the east, and he could see the green pasture and the white house with a clay tiled roof below him, and the rolling hills of forest dropping down to the wide river valley, and the high cliffs on the far side that led back to Buenos Aires. He could see the tall mountain with the cave and the eagle's perch, Marie's Mountain as he called it, to the north, and the black specks of a dozen condors soaring over the snow-capped rookery just to the west.

Then he turned around and looked at the jagged rocky peak behind him, up above the ridge where he stood, and it occurred to him that the entire valley beyond that peak, only an hour's climb if he had the mind to do it, had once belonged to him. He looked around again, down at the small white house with the pasture in front, and horses lazily grazing.

"This was all we ever needed, wasn't it, Marie?" he said. "This would have been the place we could have lived a peaceful life, and Cristian could have fished every day, and you could have had horses in the front yard, and we could have taken long rides together into the high mountain pastures."

As before, he felt sadness when he thought of what

could have been, but he was also starting to feel the same joy and amazement in this place that Marie tried so hard to share with him years before. The beauty of this place filled his senses. His eyes beheld a canvas. His ears were full of whistling wind and birdsong. His nostrils flared with the fragrance of wild mountain flowers and pine. This was a place where people really lived.

His trek down the ridge was slow and easy, stopping every so often to listen to the animals and birds, and Rocco chasing little crawling things through the leaves and trees. He'd forgotten completely about the time, and it was nearly dark when he came back around the little cabin. Pablito came from around the front, smiling and unconcerned.

"Pablito, I'm sorry, I forgot you have to take me all the way back tonight by horse."

"No, no Don Nico. Juanita has made up the white house for you tonight. There are clean sheets on the bed, and a fire is ready in the fireplace. We will take you over there when you like."

For an instant, the panic stirred in his stomach. It was a giant leap for him to stay away from home-camp for the first time in over a year. Away from the fire and the bench where Marie often came to him, away from the bed that reminded him of his son, away from everything that he thought he needed to continue to live. But as before, he drew a deep breath, and trusted his fate to his friend.

"All right, Pablito. Thank you very much.”

Pablito built the fire back up in the pit to ward off the chill, and they sat out under the clear sky and sipped a glass of wine, then another, then they walked down the trail and through the stand of trees with a full moon lighting the path. They crossed the green pasture and the horses shuffled and snorted in the shadows, and Nico could see candles lit in the window from across the field as they walked closer.

The house was built of carved stone and sealed and painted to reflect away the summer heat, and the front door was a thick Spanish style made from the rosy streaked wood of Lenga trees that live high in the mountains. Pablito opened the door and invited Nico to enter, and as he stepped in the house felt twice as big inside as it looked from outside.

It had fourteen foot tall ceilings of dark stained wood, and an enormous stone fireplace on the southern wall in the open living area, and a small but elegant kitchen off to the north with a view of the front pasture. A long hallway led to the sleeping quarters with windows that faced east for the morning sunrise.

Juanita had lit candles in the rooms and started a fire that was quickly warming the house, and prepared the bedroom for him.

"Sleep as late as you like, and we will have breakfast in the morning before we leave,” Pablito said. Then he closed the door behind him and said, "Buenas noches, my friend."

There was a small decanter of Bonarda left on the kitchen table for him, and he poured a glass and pulled one of the chairs away from the table and sat close to the fireplace for a time, with Rocco sleeping soundly by his feet.

It wasn't the strangeness of being in a home for the first time in a year that struck him, but how warm and inviting it felt. It felt like he had returned home from a long long journey. He left the glass of wine still half-full on the table and placed another log on the fire before going to bed, and he slept soundly until the rays of the sun drifted across his face through the open window.

After a breakfast of fresh bread and marmalade and hot coffee, Nico and Pablito walked from the cabin back over to the white house and gathered the horses up from their grazing in the pasture. He lifted his foot into the stirrup and grabbed the saddle loop, and with one little bounce he vaulted himself into the saddle and settled his legs around the chestnut colored mare.

He looked at the white house, and something stirred inside him. Then he turned and gazed across the pasture and down into the wide river valley where home-camp lay in the distance. He was eager to return, but something was different now; something deep inside him had shifted.

Before yesterday, he was cemented to the camp. To the place where Marie and Cristian remained, where they spoke to him in his dreams and visions. It was the place where they died, and that was the place where he felt their presence the most. Before yesterday, he thought that leaving home-camp meant leaving them behind.

But nearly every day for the past year he had been slowly drifting further and further away, and with every step, they were with him. More than that, with every step further from home-camp, their voices and their visions were sweeter, softer, and happier.

Home-camp wasn't the place where Marie and Cristian could live on in his memories and his heart. It was a place of death and tears and sadness; the most imprisoning of all human emotions. It had wrapped its arms around him like a demon and trapped him. But now he understood. Marie and Cristian lived on within him; with every step of every journey, with every laugh and smile, with every cast of the fly.

As he ventured farther away from the place of death, where he languished in misery, their hopes and dreams soared with him. As he walked the night before up to the ridge on the mountain, he felt Marie's hand in his, and heard her laughter in the wind. He felt her warmth and absolute contentment all around him, as he sat by the fireplace in the white house last night.

She was urging him to live on and take her with him. She was urging him to leave behind the man trapped by guilt and sadness, and become the man he was born to be.

As he and Pablito ambled down the trail through the monkey puzzle forest and descended to the river, he could feel the change of the seasons in the landscape. The grasses and flowers were sprouting by the hour, the river was clear and rising, the insects were hatching and fluttering in the wind, and the trout were tapping the surface with anticipation.

He could feel his own season changing too, but how it would change was as far beyond his vision as Buenos Aires beyond the eastern horizon. He knew it was somewhere out there, but he couldn't see it.

They crossed the wide vado in the river bend and took the trail to home-camp, and they could hear the cars and trucks clambering on the roadway above, and as they drew near to camp he could feel it in the depths of his soul; his time here was coming to an end. It felt comfortable and familiar, but this was not where he belonged.

As Pablito was tying the chestnut mare to his big gray, and getting ready to leave home-camp, Nico grabbed his hand and looked him in the eyes. "I don't know how to thank you for everything you've done for me, Pablito. I mean everything; not just the asado, but everything over the last year. My life is better because of you."

Pablito smiled, and pulled the old worn boina from his head and looked as if was going to say something, but then he just smiled and nodded, knowing that nothing more needed to be said. He'd seen the changes in Nico at the house this morning, and he knew things would be different from here, although he couldn't predict how. Maybe now his friend would decide to leave this place and return to the city, or somewhere else, he didn't know. But he also knew that Nico did not belong here in this sad tomb by the river bank.

He climbed up onto his big gray, and before riding away he turned and said, "You should fish today Nico. The trout are singing in the river. Maybe someday you can teach me how to fish with the magic stick that you use. I would like that." Then he wheeled the horses up river and disappeared beyond the willows.

Pandora's Box

It was nearly healed now. The long, deep scar that began at the crease of his wrist and wound in a jagged line to a point just two inches short of his elbow. The infection that festered and ached finally gave in somewhere in the midst of winter, and the scab had peeled away during his cold river washing a few days earlier. Now it looked like a lightning bolt of fresh pink skin. A badge of survival from the striking hammer of fate.

He thought Marie would have found it interesting.

He thought about her constantly, but she was coming to him less frequently now. Only occasionally whispering in his ear as he walked the hills, revealing glimpses of her face in reflections on the water, in the sky, and sometimes laughing in the flames of the fire late at night.

Even though he could still feel her near, as he did

when he walked on the ridge above the green pasture and sitting quietly by the fireplace in the white house, the physical world around him had pulled him back. He felt the irresistible call of the river and the rod, the wind and rain and glowing spring sunshine, and the company of Pablito and his family. Even the light that came to his heart through Rocco's eyes anchored him firmly to the beauty of this world where he still existed. But it made him happy to speak to her, and imagine her speaking back, if nothing else but to resist the loneliness.

He was thinking about her last night as he lay across the rear seat from the Mercedes in his little shack, staring intently at her suitcase that stood in the corner close to his bed. He sat up suddenly and said, "Marie, what did you pack for our vacation this year?"

She tilted her head and smiled, and faintly shrugged her shoulders in a whimsical "Who knows?"

It was a beautifully crafted tan leather case with matching leather straps that bound and buckled snugly, and the initials, 'MAA' for, Marie d'Auvergne de Azzarà, engraved on a silver tag that hung from the top handle. It had been sitting upright on its padded footings on top of a crate away from the dirt floor, and unopened for the past year.

It was Pandora's Box. As likely to be filled with memories and treasures, or pain and suffering for Nico if he ever dared to open it.

The tumbling in the boot of the Mercedes as it

crashed down the mountainside hadn't left a single mark on it, and having it there with him in the shack next to his bed was comforting, as if inside it were little pieces of Marie, resting near him every night when he went to sleep.

"You put something special in there, didn't you, Marie? You always brought something," he said.

"Maybe."

"I want to see it!"

"Why do you want to see it?"

"Because it must be something special and secret if you kept it locked away for this long."

"Then look, if you want."

He grabbed the bag by its handle and lifted it over to his bed and laid it flat on its side. It was heavier than he remembered.

"What's in here, Marie? It's so heavy!"

He ran his hands lightly over the case to brush away the fine desert dust, and blew the sand off the buckles, then he unclasped them and gripped the upper lid of the suitcase in his hands, and paused. This was a moment he had dreamed of for a long time, and also feared. Maybe he would find something inside this case that would bring the essence of her back to him. Or something that would consume him.

He held his breath and pushed up on the lid.

It didn't move.

The case had been closed for so long that the leather was swollen and stuck together in the seam. He pressed his knee against the handle on the bottom half and pulled up hard. The leather squeaked and popped as the lid flew open.

On top were Marie's lacy undergarments neatly folded, and several pressed blouses of different pastel shades, and beneath them in a folding soft-sided bag were her bombacha riding pants with flared boot legs and pleated high waists. She had packed two beautiful dresses for evenings in town, and two others for afternoons strolling through the gardens and shops in San Martin.

He carefully pulled the clothes out and lay them across the bed, and picked out a peached colored silk blouse, and held the soft fabric to his cheek for just a moment.

Below the soft clothes were a pair of sensible shoes and a pair of dangerously tall, patent leather heels, and black riding boots that were handcrafted for her by a leather-smith in the province of Buenos Aires. She had always adored riding, and dreamed of having a small home here in the mountains, and having her own horse to ride on warm summer days in the high mountains.

Near the bottom of the suitcase, Nico pulled out a small box that held her most favored jewelry that she always kept with her on trips. There were two pairs of long heavy earrings with dark colored jewels and small diamonds, and one pair of delicate pearl clusters in sterling silver mounts. A gold chain with a cross, inlaid with tiny rubies that she wore on Sundays to church, and a large, extravagant looking necklace made from fire coral and sapphire accents.

He remembered them all, but he couldn't remember seeing her wear them. The only visual memory he had of her was her face and flawless skin, and her long dark hair dancing in a light breeze.

Beside the jewelry box were two thick velvet bags with draw strings holding them closed. He opened the first, and pulled out a bottle of Geurlain Shalimar perfume. He held the bottle close to his nose and instantly remembered it. This was the perfume that Marie favored wearing almost every day, as had so many generations of French women for the past fifty years. The smell reminded him of the first time he took Marie to an opera in Buenos Aires, because the scent was everywhere. It also reminded him of that first night alone here by the river, and inhaling that same perfume from the inside of a plastic tarp that was draped across her lifeless body.

The second bag contained Marie's new favorite perfume for nights out with just her and Nico, Yves Saint Laurent Opium. He dabbed a small drop in the palm of his rough hand and brought it close to his face, breathed deeply and closed his eyes.

It smelled like passionate sex on a warm summer night under the open sky. Like the intimacy of moist flesh, entangling silky hair, and the musty fragrance of love.

He shuddered deep inside, and a vision of her gripped him.

Suddenly he could feel Marie's body pressed against him and her fingers running through his short wavy hair and pulling his lips more firmly against her mouth. His heart raced, and his eyes filled with tears and streamed down his cheeks. It was more than he could bear.

He jerked the perfumed hand away from his face, and lifted his head up towards the tin ceiling and opened his mouth to gasp a deep breath and pull himself back to the physical world.

He sat on the edge of the bed and wiped the salty tears away with the tail of his shirt, then looked deeper into the suitcase. In the very bottom, were two books.

The first he picked up was the one she had just purchased before they left Buenos Aires, and intended to read on lazy days while Nico was busy working. It was called, *The Old Patagonia Express*, written by Paul Theroux, about a man who ventured south from North America, all the way to Esquel in the far reach of Patagonia to find his passion for living. It still had her paper book marker in it, on page twelve.

The last thing remaining in the bottom, was Marie's secret journal.

It was a brown, leather bound booklet with a thin suede thread that came all the way around and cinched in a spiral wrapped knot. Nico held it in his hands for a few minutes, lightly rubbing his thumbs across the surface of the smooth waxed leather cover. Then, he untied the thread and opened the booklet.

He had seen her writing and drawing in it some days out on the lawn after they traveled, or after she'd been off for a day of horse riding in the mountains, but he never thought to ask what she was writing about, or why it was important to her.

It was a detail he missed in their journey together. He suspected it was mostly notes about the animals she saw during her travels across the pampas and desert and through the river valleys and mountains every year when they came to the Andes frontier, but it was much more than that.

The pages were made of fine pressed paper and stitched in the spine with braided thread, and they felt firm as he turned them from one to the next. Within the pages were not only her notes and whimsical thoughts about the amazing creatures she saw in this beautiful land, but extraordinary drawings in a level of detail and beauty that Nico had only seen in museums. Marie was as gifted an artist as she was beautiful and smart, and all these years he had never known.

He paused and studied each drawing and read her notes about the guanacos, the rheas, the red deer and the soaring condors, and at least a dozen other wild things that he had never noticed along the way. She was in love with this part of Argentina and everything that lived here, and she portrayed them in mastery with a fine charcoal pencil.

He studied the drawing she made of an animal called a Geoffrey's Cat, and she noted its aboriginal name, 'Gato Huiña', and every hair was perfectly drawn. It looked alive on the page. He continued turning the pages until he passed two that were left empty, then he arrived at something completely unexpected.

In the pages that followed were drawings that Marie made in secret, of Cristian and Nico.

The first was a sketch of Nico sleeping peacefully across a long wooden bench in the shady part of their garden in Recoleta, with his infant son laying splayed out on his chest, a pacifier in his mouth, his tiny hands clinging to Nico's shirt and his bare toes curled up like little fists.

Cristian was born in the springtime, and in the earliest months of summer Nico would often sneak away from his work to come home and have lunch with Marie. He would carry Cristian into the garden in his arms and sometimes sit on the carved bench and tell him stories about his grandfather. Some days were so warm and lazy that he would forget about work, and lay down to nap with his son in his arms.

The next was made during a day trip to the ocean, and she drew the two of them walking hand in hand down a stretch of the beach in Mar del Plata, heads down in unified concentration as they searched for treasures washed ashore by the gentle rolling waves.

"I remember that day!" Nico said out loud.

There were dozens more drawings of the two of

them together, as the bonding moments of father and son were obviously her favorite subject. As Nico turned page after page, it was like reliving the most enjoyable moments of his life over again. Some of the scenes he didn't remember, but many he did, and now they were like a gifted banquet to a starving man. Like almost all of his other assets, these memories were valuable things he possessed, but they had been misplaced or forgotten for many years.

As the memories flooded back, he also began to realize that maybe he hadn't been such an abandoning father after all. Since the day their car fell from the mountain he was consumed with the guilt of unfulfilled promises he made to Cristian, and the more gentle and generous moments they shared were repressed from his sight. Now he had them back, in the most lovingly portrayed message that Marie could offer.

It was more than just the journal that Marie kept secret all these years; it was the heart and soul of an artist that she kept safely hidden from the world and everyone she knew.

"Why would you hide this, Marie?" he said. But there was no answer in his mind.

Marie watched in silence those years while Nico suppressed his passion for a life in the outdoors and for the joy he felt when he was on the river with his father and friends. Then again when he lost himself in the struggle to prove himself worthy. Her father spent fortunes on education and training to groom her for a life in the upper class, and she thought that was what Nico expected of her too, so she didn't resist. How could she disappoint them by chasing a silly dream of her own. No, it was a dream best kept in secret, she thought.

Nico pushed his own dreams aside and allowed his fears and resentment to drive his life forward. It brought him success and wealth, but he was paying a price he never realized, and it was a heavy price. A price of losing the closeness and memories and time spent together in a brief and fleeting existence. But love has no price.

Love is a bond not easily broken by fear or envy, time or distance, or even death; and despite the price Nico paid all those years in search of riches, the love he felt for Marie and Cristian never waned. In the months before, Nico believed that he had lost everything, that nothing remained of his former life. But Marie had shown him the truth, that he still possessed the most valuable thing in all the world, a love so strong that it penetrates the barriers of space and time.

He closed Marie's journal and laid it on his lap, and looked at the orange glow of sunrise coming through the thin tent covering on the door. A smile of contentment came across his face as he realized just how wealthy he still was, and he said to her, "Marie, my love for you is stronger than the grip of death that keeps us apart. Love will bind me to you, wherever you are."

An Old Friend

It was late in the day, nearly time to build the afternoon fire, when Rocco alerted him to danger. He was staring up at the pullout on the highway, and mumbling a low growl. Nico looked up at the road and could clearly make out a green truck with the markings of the Gendarmerie and a silver colored sedan parked by the road. A lone man was walking across the worn path from the highway coming towards home-camp. His first instinct was to run, but where would he run to? He decide it better to face whatever was coming with calm.

As the man drew nearer, his walk and movement, everything about him was infinitely familiar, it was Jorge. His mind raced with a thousand notions of his impending demise, but again, he decided to stay calm and face his former friend. Rocco sensed Nico's fear and anger, and his warning growl grew louder as Jorge came closer to the camp. "Shhh, easy boy."

"Am I welcome?" Jorge said as he came through the brush and into the camp.

"That depends," Nico responded. "Are they here for me?" he said, as he glanced up at the Gendarmerie.

"They've always been here for you," Jorge said. "Colonel Lopez has been watching for a long time, just to make sure you were ok. On days when the bus lines didn't come past here, his men would stop and make sure there was food left up there for you. He's been calling me every week for the last six months to let me know that you were still alive, and that you were fishing most days up the river and looked healthy. He's been a friend to you here when I couldn't be."

Nico was taken aback. He never considered in all this time that others were watching out for him. "You knew about the bus drivers leaving me food?" he said.

"I was paying them to leave you food. Whenever they had a route coming past they were supposed to drop off some sandwiches and simple food, and maybe a bottle of wine from time to time."

"What about the black sedan, who were they?" he said.

"They belonged to Jacques," Jorge said with a serious tone. "We have a lot to talk about. Is it safe for me to tell the officers up there they can leave me alone with you? You're not going to kill me, right?" Then he smiled and the tense look on his face relaxed.

"You're safe, I'm in no mood to fight today," Nico said.

"I'm going to get a few things from my car, and tell them it's ok to leave now," Jorge said. Then he started the long hike back to the road.

Rocco felt the tension slipping away from Nico's posture and his expression, and he sat calmly on his haunches but never took his eyes away from Jorge as he walked back to the roadway. Nico's mind was still swirling with the revelations that Jorge and the Gendarmerie were protecting him and feeding him this whole time, and his sense of time was still contorted.

On the one hand, it felt like he'd only been here since yesterday because his visions of Marie and Cristian were still so strong and his memories of the accident so vivid. But in another way, it felt like he had been in this place, this beautiful mountainous wilderness and the river valley, for his entire life.

He gathered up twigs and sticks, and by the time Jorge came back to camp with a large backpack over his shoulder, the fire was burning well and he piled on a few large branches.

"I brought my fly rod, do you feel like fishing for dinner?" Jorge said, as he walked in and set his pack on the ground.

"Looks like you plan on staying," Nico said, looking at Jorge's pack.

"I thought I might do some spring fishing, and

hoped you wouldn't mind if I camped here for a day or two. Come on, show me how to fish your river," he said.

Nico could see an evening hatch of spring mayflies was just beginning to flutter in the breeze as they walked to the river an hour later. "Show me what flies you brought with you," he said to Jorge.

Jorge stopped and pulled out his polished wooden fly box and handed it to Nico, and he opened it and carefully inspected the flies.

"These are all wrong. You don't have anything that matches what the trout are getting ready to eat."

He tossed the box back to Jorge, then reached into his ragged shirt pocket and pulled out three flies, and chose one and handed it to him. "Use this," he said.

Jorge looked at the worn fly, and it had barely any hackle and hair left on it and the hook was rusty and the barb cut off. It looked like a fly that he would have thrown in the trash years ago.

"Are you sure? This isn't much of a fly, and the barb is gone. How am I going to keep a fish on the hook, even if one takes this grubby thing?"

"That fly has been feeding me for the past six months. I pinched down the barb because I care more about the fish in this river than your ego. A good fisherman can land a fish without a barb," he said with a sneer. "Use it, or don't. It makes no difference to me. Start fishing up there on the first bend. Make three casts close to the shoreline, then start working your way farther out into the river, a few feet at a time. Cover all the water well. You can't see it this time of year, but there's a rock shelf in the middle of that bend, and the trout stack up below and wait for insects that wash down the river."

Jorge nodded and smiled as he turned up river and walked to the place Nico suggested. He could feel Nico's mastery of the river and didn't doubt his word when it came to fishing. He wasn't yet convinced about his sanity, but when it came to fishing he knew Nico was born to be a river-god.

Before Jorge settled into his casting spot at the bend, Nico was already bringing his first rainbow trout to hand thirty yards down stream. On Jorge's third cast and drift along the bend, a beautiful brown trout came to the surface and gulped the rusty worn fly, and over the next half hour it raised a half dozen more fish to the surface. Jorge and Nico glanced back and forth at each other from a distance and smiled or mocked each other as they landed or lost fish, but never exchanged words. It was more a moment of re-bonding.

In a short time, the calm of the river washed away everything but the connection the two men had shared since they were boys. As they walked back to camp, Jorge cut the rusty fly loose from his line and offered it back to Nico, "You were right, as usual," he said.

"Keep it. It might save your life one day," Nico said with a smile.

They hung the trout over the fire pit to cook, and Jorge reached into his pack and pulled out a bottle of wine and pulled the cork, then filled two plastic cups and handed one to Nico. Then he held up his cup and said, "To starting life over."

Nico paused at the toast, and considered the depth of the words. Then he nodded and tapped his cup to Jorge's, and they drank, and were silent in their own thoughts.

As the fish started to sizzle, Nico started the conversation. "So tell me about Jacques."

Jorge began, "We were all worried that you were losing your mind, but Jacques...Jacques was the one who went over the edge. After the funeral, all he could think about was revenge. It consumed him. He had one of his lawyer friends arrange for thugs to watch you, and they tried to make your life tougher by robbing you of whatever they could. Their orders were to leave you with nothing but the shirt on your back, and to take that too if they could get it. But you messed that plan up."

"I messed up his face along with it."

"The one you beat the shit out of, ended up in the hospital in Neuquen, and he started talking about pressing charges against you, but the Gendarmerie got involved and they got to the truth of it. He confessed that he'd been hired by some city lawyer to do it. It all went straight back to Jacques."

"Did anything happen to Jacques?"

"Colonel Lopez called me to let me know what was going on, and that he had men watching out for you;

but we decided it wasn't worth pursuing anything against Jacques. He was a lonely old man who had lost his daughter and his only grandson, and his mind betrayed him. We've known Jacques for years, and he wasn't a bad man, he was just broken. When men are faced with a thing like that, they do and say things they don't really mean. Things that don't reflect who they really are."

They sat silently for a moment, then Nico said, "So you expect me to apologize for breaking your arm?"

He stared blankly at Jorge, then eased into a smile that betrayed his bluff and his embarrassment.

"I'll say sorry after you tell me if I'm completely broke now or if there's at least something left to start my life over with."

Then he looked across the river valley into the blazing sunset, and poked at the fire to stir the coals back to flame. "I'm ready to move on now, Jorge. But I don't know how to leave this place. This river valley feels more like home to me than anyplace I've ever been, and this is where Marie and Cristian live in my heart."

"Then don't leave, Nico," Jorge said calmly.

"But it won't be long before whoever owns this land is going to get tired of having me squatting here, and he'll force Pablito to make me leave, or just send the police to do it."

"Nico, it's all taken care of. I suppose it's time I tell

you what I've been doing with all your money," Jorge said.

Nico's head came up suddenly and he stared into Jorge's eyes with a flash of dread.

"I knew from the first day I found you here on this river bank, that everything you loved and cared about in this world was here, not back in Buenos Aires. There is nothing back there for you."

Then Jorge pulled the wool blanket a little tighter around his shoulders and braced himself for what he was about to say to his best friend.

"Nico, I've sold off most of the businesses in Buenos Aires. The lumber mill, and the big furniture company. If I hadn't done it, Jacques and his financiers would have ruined the market and the businesses would have gone bankrupt. I got rid of the companies before they became worthless, and as it turned out, Jacques went broke trying to get his revenge on you."

"What?!" "How could you do that to me? That company was what I dreamed about!"

"No Nico, that was just what you worked at doing to get yourself off the streets. Everything you ever dreamed of is right here. We've been best friends since we were boys, remember? I know you better than anyone. So let me finish, then if you want to fire me, or kill me, you can."

"There's more?" Nico said.

"Yes." Jorge said, nodding and staring directly into his friend's eyes with a confident smile.

"After I sold the lumber mill and Azzarà Industries, I started acquiring other small bits of land. A few hundred acres here, and a few thousand there. It took me a long time to convince some of the land owners to sell, but eventually they agreed when they realized what I was doing."

Jorge raised his arm and pointed to the south across the river to the peak that looks down on the white house and green pasture and Pablito's puesto, and said, "You see that mountain? Your timber estancia lies in the valley on the other side and backs up to that peak. I kept that land because it makes good profit from just growing wild and being beautiful; and because Marie and Cristian always loved that place more than any other."

Nico sighed lightly with relief that he still owned the timberland.

"What you own now, is everything on this side of that mountain as well, down to the river valley and across to the high peak on this side of the river, including the land you're squatting on now. You've been living on your own land for the past few months. Pablito won't run you off, because he works for you, but he doesn't know that yet."

Nico's mouth fell open, and he felt his heart racing and his eyes starting to swell. He turned his head to the western horizon again to keep Jorge from seeing the tears streaming down his face, and he raised his arm and pulled the sleeve from his shirt to blot the tears.

Then Jorge continued, "The man who inherited most of that property was an old acquaintance of Jacques, and he got burned badly in Jacques' scheme to corner the lumber and furniture manufacturing industry. He never cared much about this ranch land, and when he came in need of cash after the investing fiasco he agreed to sell it. It was that last big parcel we needed. So in a way, Jacques was responsible for you owning this entire valley."

Nico sat quietly, trying to process everything he was hearing, but it wasn't sinking in yet. "So let me ask you something else. The truck that lost all the roofing tin and plywood on the curve up there last fall. That was you, wasn't it?" Nico asked.

"Of course," Jorge said. He grinned and turned away to keep from laughing.

"You might have had it land a little closer, you know. I nearly broke my back trying to pull all of it down that mountainside and build a shelter here!"

"You were being an ass. That was payback," Jorge said. Then he reached over and poured another sip of wine into Nico's cup, and into his own.

Nico sat for a few minutes without speaking; just staring at the western sky across the wide river valley that he now knew belonged completely to him, and searched for his next words.

"What can I do here, Jorge?" Nico whispered.

"Do what your heart has been wanting to do your whole life, Nico. Build something wonderful to share your passion for the wild river, and the fish, and the joy you've always felt when you're standing in the current and casting in the wind. Make this a magical place where people from all over the world want to come and share your dream. And don't worry about the money, there's plenty put aside to build it, and the timber estancia makes enough to pay for it for the rest of your lifetime."

Then Jorge continued, "Nico, Patagonia is starting to grow, but it needs people who really understand it, to show it to the world. Right now there are thousands of people leaving Buenos Aires to settle in San Carlos de Bariloche, and some to San Martin de Los Andes. The ski resorts are growing, and there are even a few foreign fly fishermen starting to come here. This place is a paradise, and you could be the man who shows it to the world."

Jorge stood up and said, "I'll be back in a few minutes, I need to get something else from the car." Then he headed off across the brushy hillside with a small flashlight to navigate his way.

Nico sat and stared at the flames, and felt a peaceful warmth surrounding him. This place on the river had been his own little personal hell for a while, the place he used to torment and punish himself. But suddenly it felt different, like the world, and Marie and Cristian were all smiling and telling him it was time to find happiness again. Rocco got up from his place by the warm fire and came over with his tail wagging and licked Nico's cheek.

Then curled up next to his thigh and groaned with contentment.

He could see the little beam of light darting back and forth through the darkness and hear Jorge cursing the thorns as he got closer, then he emerged from the darkness and came to the fire light holding a long wooden box. It was the bamboo rod built so many years ago by his father, Gerard, for a prince in Belgium who would never receive it.

"Nico, when we were young all you ever talked about was being able to fish with this rod someday. Then after your father died you refused to even take it out of the box and handle it because you said it was too valuable. Your father didn't spend months of his life working on this fly rod so that it could end up in a museum or someone's closet after he died. He made it to be used and enjoyed. It has a purpose and you've been denying it all these years," Jorge said.

"But what if it breaks? It won't be worth anything anymore," Nico said.

"Nico, this isn't an asset or an investment, it's an instrument of joy. It brings the most value to the man who uses it and appreciates it for what it is. Your father would want you to use it and prove to the world just how great he really was when he made it. You and this rod are the two best things your father left to this world, he would want you both to fulfill your destiny."

"I'll think about it, Jorge," Nico said. Then he stood up and started walking towards the little shack with the box in his hands. "Thank you for bringing this to me, I forgot it was still locked away."

Nico spent that night dreaming about his father. They were peaceful dreams about when he was a boy, and in the dream Nico was a boy too, running and playing with his father along the rivers and streams in the Italian countryside. He couldn't really remember it, because he was very young when they left Italy, and it had been too dangerous during the war years to travel off into the woods to fish or explore, but in his dream they were free to do what young boys do.

In the dream his father cut a fresh willow branch and fashioned a magical rod that they used to catch trout after trout in a rocky stream, and as the dream came to an end, his father handed the willow-branch rod to him and said, "This is for you. It will always bring you luck."

He woke the next morning with his father's voice still ringing in his ears, and an unquenchable desire to be on the river with a rod in his hands. He sat up and reached for the box that held the bamboo fly rod, and pulled it to his lap and untied the two leather clasps, and opened it.

He lifted the lower handle section of the bamboo rod from the case and admired the olive wood reel seat and engraved silver locking rings that held the reel in place. He ran his fingertips over the floral patterned cork handle that came from ancient trees in France, where they carefully harvested the cork bark only once after twenty years of growth.

The rod itself was made from a special bamboo cane that was imported before the war from the southern most region of China, and his father split it into slender sections with only his hands and a small razor sharp wedge. He spent weeks carefully shaping six long pieces to fit together in a perfect hexagon, then glued them and bound them tightly with coarse thread and left it to cure for 28 days in a warm and shaded room of his house.

When he took the bindings off, he began the slow process of sanding and shaving nodules and bumps and imperfections from the surface. He created a perfect taper to the tip, so the rod would flex smoothly just beyond the center, and have a tip that was so sensitive he could feel even the slightest tick, but strong enough to hold against a powerful fish.

The silver rings that guided the line down the length of the rod were wrapped in place with blue and gold thread and sealed with clear lacquer, and the large one at the base had a ruby colored crystal insert. On the butt of the handle was a silver plate, with the letter "A" engraved, for *Azzarà*. It was a masterpiece of rod craft, and the last expression of what Gerard had most treasured doing in his lifetime.

Nico was still wealthy it seemed, and not just in the ways of money. He had a vision of how his wealth might serve the world around him. He wasn't wandering without purpose anymore, he could see a clear horizon.

As he held his father's masterpiece in his hands, he felt the confidence of a man who no longer has need of his voice to announce himself to the world. He had moved fully into his own ethereal realm. There was only one demon remaining that needed to be faced.

He stepped out into the early morning light and found Jorge cooking breakfast over the fire pit. He sat on Marie's bench, and Jorge poured a fresh cup of steaming coffee into a tin cup and handed it to him.

"Jorge, did you bring more fishing flies with you?" he asked after a few moments.

"Of course! You don't think I'd come all the way here without new flies."

"I need something special. Let me take a look at what you brought," Nico said.

Jorge rummaged through his pack and pulled a wooden fly box out and handed it to Nico, and he opened it and studied all of the little flies carefully, but shook his head. "What I need isn't in here, but I think I can make it if I take some of these apart and use the materials together. Do you mind?" he asked.

"What are you going to make?" Jorge asked.

"Something big. Really big."

Nico was so completely in tune with the river and the land that he knew from day to day and moment to moment what creatures and insects were hatching and moving, and what the trout were feeding on. All around the hillside and the river's edge, the bamboo cane was coming to its twelve year cycle of flowering and death. He knew this was the time when the large mice came to gorge on the seeds of the cane, then they would go to the river to drink after filling their bellies to the point of bursting.

The oldest and largest of the trout in the river were also aware, and they would be waiting along the river's edge in the twilight hours for the fattened mice and rats that would surely fall into the swift current. This would be Nico's chance to draw the demon fish from the depths of the channel.

He pulled out half a dozen large streamer flies from the box that were all made from brown deer hair, and started cutting them apart and piling the hair into one large bundle, and saving the thread to wind it back together onto a single large hook. He worked for two hours to bind it and tie it together, then used the small scissors on his knife tool to meticulously carve and shape the bundle into the crude form of a little mouse. Then he tied a long leather strip on the end for a tail that would wiggle from behind as it swam through the water.

Then he waited. Waited for three days. On the second day, the bamboo cane along the upper river began to blossom, and after lunch on the third day he spotted the first swollen mouse carcass floating down along the edge of the shoreline. The big carnivorous fish would be feeding soon.

As the late afternoon insect hatch started swarming along the tree line, Jorge grabbed his rod and turned to Nico. "Are you ready to catch dinner?"

"You go ahead. I'll be going to the river later," he said.

Jorge looked confused. It was the perfect time to fish, just as they'd been doing for several days. But he didn't question anything about fishing when it came to Nico, so he walked to the river by himself, and enjoyed his afternoon fishing in the same place as the days before.

He came back into camp after the sun had fallen below the mountain peaks to the west. A full moon was slowly rising on the eastern horizon at the same time like a planetary scale shifting its balance around the world. He had two nice trout for the fire to feed him and Nico, and one for Rocco, who had a grand taste for fresh trout by this time.

"The trout were really biting this afternoon!" he said. "No big fish though, all medium size, but perfect for eating. Sorry you weren't there with me."

"I'll be going out later. I'm just waiting for the right time," Nico said.

They ate dinner by the fire and sipped the last bit of wine, and chatted about Pablito and the white house and green pasture, as the full moon slid overhead. The magnitude of Jorge's news about owning the entire valley was slowly sinking in, and Nico was starting to envision himself moving into the white house.

He couldn't think of anyplace he would rather be living, and Marie's spirit would always be with him there. He also had friends that felt more like family already living next door, and Pablito and Juanita and the girls would always be there for him. It was like all the stars in the sky were starting to shine just for him.

All through the night as they sat and talked, Nico was listening for the sounds of the river. He was waiting for the tune that would call him to come. At 12:30 he moved over to Cristian's bench for a clear view of the water in the moonlight, and his search for the signs became more intense.

Jorge was starting to get sleepy, but he wasn't about to miss whatever was about to happen. He could see the intent on Nico's face changing as the night wore on. Then came a loud 'splash'. And a few moments later another, and the sound of small fish fleeing and breaking the surface. He saw another crash on the far bank and the spray of water into the light, and he knew it was time.

By this time, Nico was sitting on the bench with the bamboo rod laying across his lap, already tied with the mouse fly and ready for battle. He stood and started a slow stalk down the bank in the darkness, and as Jorge stood up behind him he turned, "Stay here Jorge. I need to do this alone."

He made a slow creep in the shadows, one foot gliding in front of the other. No sudden movements to give away his position with the moonlight shining overhead. He came to the river far down stream from where the big demon lived and moved up along the rocks until he came to a large boulder on the edge.

Nico wanted make his assault from here rather than wading into the river where the demon would surely sense his presence. He climbed barefooted to the top and kneeled to keep a low profile, and pulled out line from the reel to make his cast. He made a false cast into the darkness, sending the huge mouse forward over the shoreline first, then drew it back through the air one more time to gain more power, and launched it across the river to the far cut-bank.

He couldn't see it in the night shadows, but he heard it land with a thump against the muddy bank, and he let it sit motionless for a few seconds. Then he pulled it into the water with a quick jerk. The flowing river grabbed the mouse and washed it downstream in the current, and he jerked it twice more to make it look like a panicked swimming rodent that had fallen into the water.

In the midst of his second strip of the mouse fly, the night exploded into chaos. He pointed the elegant bamboo rod to the crashing sound in the water and pulled the line back in his left hand with all his might, and when the needle sharp hook buried deep into the demon's jaw, it wheeled over and smashed its tail on the surface and dove deep into the channel.

The surge nearly ripped the rod from Nico's grip, but his hands were as strong as a vice. As the fish went deep, Nico pulled the rod up and to the side to turn his head, and the bamboo bowed over into an arch and bucked in his hands as the fish thrashed his giant head, but the rod never made a squeak or a creak or threatened to break.

With his dive to the deep foiled, the fish turned upriver and raced against the current, making the reel sing as the line peeled away. But this fish was no fool, and when he'd taken fifty yards of line from the reel he wheeled again and charged straight back at Nico with the swift current at his back.

The line went slack as Nico tried desperately to strip the line with his hand and bring it tight again, and as the line went limp in the water the big demon showed his face in the moonlight. He broke the surface in a rush and soared six feet into the night sky. His gaping mouth swinging from side to side trying to shake the hook free, and those evil black cat eyes glaring at Nico as he twisted and spun through the air in a cartwheel and nearly emptied the river when he landed in a crushing flop.

The acrobatics nearly threw the hook loose, but they gave Nico the instant he needed to pull the line tight again, and furrow the hook even deeper behind the demon's rows of teeth. With the hook firmly set, it was now a test of strength between the bamboo rod, and the power of the fish.

The war raged up and down the current, with Nico staying high atop the boulder, pivoting back and forth to keep pressure on the fish until he had nothing left. But when the big fish finally weakened and came close to the boulder, Nico realized he had no way to land him. Then out of the darkness came a crashing into the river, and a wide net lunging forward under the giant fish and upward, and his heavy body folded into the webbing as it came up.

There in moonlight, chest deep in the freezing river with the shock of cold and excitement across his face, was Jorge.

"I couldn't stay out of the fight!" he yelled.

Nico threw his head back and laughed as he hadn't done in a long time. "I'm glad you didn't!"

He climbed down from the boulder to take the net from Jorge and confront his demon, face to face. He held the net barely in the water and reached in to pull the mouse from the demon's jaw, and stared into those eyes that haunted his dreams.

During the entire battle in the darkness he was thinking about killing and eating this evil beast, but as he looked into those eyes being lit by the full moon overhead, he saw nothing evil in them. This magnificent creature wasn't evil, he was just ancient.

Born as a small fry like millions of others, he had lasted through the ages by doing as nature meant him to do. Feeding, fighting, and surviving with his instincts kept him alive in this river as long as Nico had been alive himself. He had grown into a river-god. An ethereal. And now his life lay in the hands of the only one who had ever defeated him.

Nico sat back in the rushing river, and felt a wave of compassion coming over him. No, not compassion. Respect and admiration. He held the giant brown trout gently by the tail and faced him into the current as the water brought reviving oxygen over his gills, and he cradled him there for a long time. He felt the life force coming slowly back to his sleek body, and when he felt strong enough, Nico unleashed his grip and slid the mighty fish back into the depths without a word.

Nico stood up in the water and turned to look at Jorge, who's face was beaming in the moonlight in its usual way. He grabbed him in a bear hug, and slapped his back and said, "Let's have a drink."

No sleep was had that night. The two friends uncorked a bottle of Irish whiskey and were still telling stories and making plans for the river valley, when the sun came up over Buenos Aires and slid over the desert horizon. More than one demon had been conquered this night.

The Patagonian

The shuffling and impatient pawing and stomping outside let Nico know it was time for the morning carrots. He grabbed two large ones from a woven basket on the kitchen counter and opened the front door of the house and stepped outside, and was greeted by his appaloosa mare, who was heavy with foal, and a criollo gelding that liked to have his neck scratched early in the morning before receiving his carrot. He went out into the green pasture with Rocco bouncing ahead and handed each horse their treat, then smiled as he looked across the river valley, and thought of *her*.

The last year of living here in the little white house had been filled with joy and purpose, and still, some days brought the expected longing and sadness. He knew those feelings would never leave him, but he molded them into his passion for living on, and creating a life that would make her smile.

Nico wanted the world to remember Marie for who she really was, and for the things she loved. After settling into the house, he went straight to work on a series of plans.

The first came to life in a beautiful stone building on the outskirts of San Martin de Los Andes. It was once a private home, built in the previous century from river stone taken from the nearby Chimehuin River, and had a large open foyer with well preserved wood floors, and a staircase leading to the second floor where all of the four bedrooms had been. For over one hundred years, it had been filled with the laughter of children and grandchildren, as three generations lived and grew together, before Europe called for the sons to come for the second great war, and none returned. It fell empty when the last of the family died.

Nico bought the homestead and restored the first floor to its original state, and opened the entire upper floor into a large gallery. He added lighting in the appropriate spaces, and several comfortable benches throughout the floorspace. The sign above the front door read, "Marie d'Auvergne Arts Center", and it held a permanent exhibit of twenty nine drawings by Marie that were carefully reproduced and enlarged, and perfectly framed and hung about the gallery.

Every other month, the gallery hosted a new young talented artist, and kept their work on display for the thousands of visitors coming through town every year. On the day of the grand opening, exactly two years from the day of her passing, Nico stood at the front of a large crowd. There were people from San Martin, people from Buenos Aires, and people from the cultural centers and art galleries about South America in attendance, as Jacques d'Auvergne proudly cut the ribbon to the entrance, and welcomed them in to see his daughter's legacy.

After the art center was opened, Nico began work on the new lodge that would sit above the mesa looking over the river. Constructed in true mountain style from Oregon pine and stone, it would be the first grand destination resort for world traveling fly fishermen in the Patagonian Andes.

It would become a place where men and women, kings and common, and all manner of people would gather to celebrate their love of the rod and the fly, and the great beastly trout that filled the rivers in this part of the world. Even the president of Argentina came every summer to fish with old friends and share a glass of wine on the terrace under the stars.

Nico ventured down to the wide vado on the Limay and waded across sometimes to lay a flower at the base of the white marble monument that stood where the little glittering gem-filled rock had once been. The rock now rested in the flower garden, outside the little white house on the hill.

Sometimes in the early evening he would hear the

small fish racing and fleeing in the deep channel under the willows, and he knew the old brown trout still held sway over his world beneath the waves. And every year on the same day, Nico gathered his pack behind the saddle of his horse, and he and Rocco went alone to home-camp.

He built a fire, and caught two trout with the rod made for a prince, and hung them over the spit on a fresh willow branch. He would spend the whole night sitting on the wood bench, wrapped tightly against the cool night air and Rocco curled around his feet, and patiently wait for the first falling star of summer to streak across the sky in a flaming green descent.

What Did You Think?

Thank you for reading ***Where The Green Star Falls***.

If you liked it, I have a favor to ask. Like all other authors these days, my success depends entirely on you. Your opinions and thoughts about the book are all that matter. People want to know what you think.

Please take a minute and share your thoughts in a review. As little or as much as you feel like writing would be great. You can help make this book a success.

Just sign in to your retailer account, go to the sales page for ***Where The Green Star Falls***, and follow the easy instructions to leave a review near the bottom of the page.

Thank You!

William Jack Stephens

Also by William Jack Stephens

* * *

Where The Green Star Falls

* * *

Andalusian Legacy

* * *

Mallorca Vendetta

* * *

Emissary of Vengeance

About the Author

Novelist and adventure writer, Jack has lived and explored the world from the Arctic to the southern reaches of Patagonia.

In his former life, he served in executive roles with some of the largest companies in the world. Now he writes gripping and inspirational tales of adventure, and the occasional love story.

In South America he's known by his Spanish nickname, Memo, and when he's not writing, he can usually be found on a wilderness river with a fly rod in his hands.

www.williamjackstephens.com
jack@williamjackstephens.com

Dedication

Where The Green Star Falls is dedicated to the extraordinary men and women who live, work, and play in the vast wilderness of Patagonia, Argentina.

* * *

Where The Green Star Falls is a work of fiction. Names, characters, businesses, places, events and incidents are either the products of the author's imagination or used in a fictitious manner. Any resemblance to actual persons, living or dead, or actual events is purely coincidental.

ASIN: B076VS49Y9

ISBN 9781973134558

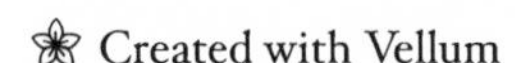
Created with Vellum